once in a
full moon

ALSO BY ELLEN SCHREIBER

ELLEN SCHREIBER

once in a
full moon

KATHERINE TEGEN BOOKS
An Imprint of HarperCollinsPublishers

To my dad, who always liked werewolves,
and to my husband, Eddie, for romantic strolls in the moonlight

HarperTeen is an imprint of HarperCollins Publishers.
Katherine Tegen Books is an imprint of HarperCollins Publishers.

Once in a Full Moon
Copyright © 2011 by Ellen Schreiber

Library of Congress Cataloging-in-Publication Data
Schreiber, Ellen.
    Once in a full moon / Ellen Schreiber. — 1st ed.
       p.   cm.
    Summary: Popular seventeen-year-old Celeste finds herself falling in love with
a boy from the wrong side of their small, midwestern town, even though she sus-
pects that he is a werewolf.
    ISBN 978-0-06-198650-5 (trade bdg.)
    [1. Supernatural—Fiction. 2. Popularity—Fiction. 3. Dating (Social cus-
toms)—Fiction. 4. High schools—Fiction. 5. Schools—Fiction. 6. Werewolves—Fiction.] I. Title.
PZ7.S3787Onc 2011
[Fic]—dc22
                 2010018359
                 CIP
                 AC

Typography by Amy Ryan
11 12 13 14 15 LP/RRDB 10 9 8 7 6 5 4 3 2 1
❖
First Edition

CONTENTS

"Beware of a kiss under the full moon.
It will change your life forever."
—Dr. Camille Meadows

once in a
full moon

ONE

harvest moon

It began underneath the haunting glow of a full moon.

I was deep within the woods with my boyfriend, Nash, my best friends, Ivy and Abby, and their boyfriends, Jake and Dylan, all of us huddled around a campfire and telling ghost stories. It was unusual for us to venture off into nature, as we spent most of our time in the safety of suburbia. The guys were acting brave, but we girls were cringing with fear. We were totally isolated—no hikers or campers were anywhere in sight. The fire pit and a few flashlights were our only sources of light in the dark night. I was snuggled against Nash, Abby was holding her boyfriend Dylan's hand, and Jake had his arm around Ivy. The logs crackled and the heat from the fire kept us warm in the crisp, late-autumn air.

"This is so freaky," Ivy whispered to me. "I still can't

believe you convinced us to come out here. There isn't a store for miles."

Ivy was out of her element and doing her best to assuage her discomfort by sipping a latte and snuggling up to Jake.

"If only it wasn't so dark," Abby said, stretching out her long, lean legs on a blanket. "We could hike, too."

"I can think of better things to do in the dark than hike," Dylan said, tickling her waist.

"That's the whole point," I said. "Isn't it more romantic, underneath the moon and stars?"

With winter approaching, it was only going to become darker and colder, and I wanted to take advantage of being outdoors with my friends.

"Romantic?" Ivy sighed. "I'm cold, in the middle of nowhere, and frightened to death by these ghost stories. This is your idea of romantic?"

I didn't have to respond. She already knew.

"Of course it is." Ivy grinned. "Always the dreamer! I guess that's why you're my best friend."

"Hey!" Abby said, sitting up.

Ivy and I had been best friends before Abby joined our clique. Sometimes Ivy forgot her manners.

"I meant to say best *friends*," Ivy corrected. "You both are."

"Catfight!" Dylan said. "Let me record this." He brandished his cell, but Abby was over Ivy's slipup as soon as Ivy gave her an apologetic hug.

"Anyway," I said to Abby, excited that I might have stirred

up some interest. "Maybe we can come here again during the day for a hike."

She gave me two enthusiastic thumbs-up.

"Let's get through the next few hours," Nash said, finishing his s'more, "before we plan on any further 'Celeste Parker excursions.'"

Normally I would have rolled my eyes at Nash's playful jab, but I was grateful that my boyfriend and his posse finally gave in to my suggestion for date night.

I'd been suggesting outdoor activities that didn't involve an opposing team or a goalpost for ages. I wasn't an avid outdoorsy type or anything, but I did prefer to do other things with my friends besides going shopping or watching sports. The reason the guys were game was the promise of food and the potential of scaring three girls to death.

"Well, I think we should listen to Celeste more often," Jake said, devouring the last Rice Krispies treat I'd made for our outing.

My friends acted as if I possessed superpowers for making the simplest of snacks.

Shadows danced menacingly against the trees. The October night skies of the midwestern town of Legend's Run were beautiful. Stars glimmered like ten-carat diamonds. I'd have wished on one that this night would never end, but I'd settle for savoring the memories when I recorded these moments in my worn-out spiral notebook journal: the fresh air, my best friends giggling by my side, my date holding my hand.

Nash squeezed me extra tight. I wasn't sure if it was because he was truly having fun or if, instead, he was wondering what he was going to gain by agreeing to this experience. He knew better than to press me too hard, but that didn't stop him from trying. Nash massaged my fingers and wrists and I was in heaven. I returned his smile. It was a spectacular night.

"This is awesome," I said. "We must do this again. See? I do have great ideas."

"Yes, great," Nash concurred. Then he whispered so only I could hear: "And we could make this night even greater."

Like most girls in Legend's Run, I'd had a crush on Nash since I could remember. He had handsome good looks and eyes that twinkled, and he possessed an air of confidence that made him stand out among our schoolmates. But behind his charming ways was a hint of insecurity. For me, I was almost as attracted to the possibility that he was not as confident as he appeared as I was to his appearance and his playfulness.

Nash leaned in for a kiss and I melted against his lips. For a moment I lost track of where we were, until I heard my friends snickering. I lowered my chin and reached up to fix my hair and he reluctantly backed off.

It was wonderful having my friends around me, and the attention from Nash was flattering. We were finally away from the cheering crowds, girls vying for him, or winning-obsessed coaches who normally surrounded Nash, the star athlete at our school. It was unusual for Nash to be focused on life beyond sports, so I cherished our perfect night together. Feeling like a lone wolf who prefers the companionship of the wolf pack, I felt safe in our clique. I'd never been as happy in our group as I was tonight. I took pride knowing my friends were having fun hanging outside their comfort zone, and I enjoyed knowing Nash wanted to hold me more than a stitched leather ball.

"This is how it should always be," Ivy said. "The six of us together." She raised her latte for a toast. "Forever."

We all grabbed our hot coffees and raised them toward the moon.

"Forever?" Nash groaned. "That's a long time."

I wasn't shaken by his remark. Rather, it stirred something I'd been feeling, too. Was Nash the kind of guy I wanted to be together with forever? Could I really see myself with someone who was usually more devoted to himself and to sports than others, when this is what caused us to be part-time now?

I gazed at my friends, who seemed so enamored with their dates. I couldn't imagine anything breaking their bonds. I envied them.

"Wow—that full moon," Abby said. "It's haunting, isn't it?"

"Speaking of full moons," Nash said, hopping to his feet. "It's my turn to tell a scary story, and this one is *real*."

Nash, handsome with his boyishly beautiful features and muscular build, took center stage behind the fire as if the small flames were footlights. He began telling a story of a werewolf in Legend's Run in the early 1900s.

I scooted next to Ivy, who linked her bony arm with mine as if it were a designer purse.

"Many years ago, as the full moon shown bright," Nash said with an eerie tone, "the inhabitants of Legend's Run heard a horrible howling. The cry of the beast wailed throughout the town. As the howling grew closer, children woke up from their sleep, travelers had to control their horses, and homeowners locked their doors. The few brave souls who did venture out to investigate say they witnessed a creature never seen before—a monster standing on two legs, thin as a man, hairy as a dog, with the fangs of a wolf and the eyes of a beast."

"Ooh!" Ivy whimpered, hugging my arm.

Tall tales of werewolves ran rampant for generations in Legend's Run. It might have been because occasionally a wolf was spotted in the outlying wooded areas and in the early days there wasn't much else to do but create outlandish stories of their origin. I was a skeptic on rumors; I had the mindset that I'd have to see it to believe it. To me, there was a big line between fact and fantasy. However, hanging out here in the darkness, anything seemed possible.

"The creature appeared tormented," he continued. "It was ready to attack at any moment." Nash raised his hands as if he were the monster.

Now I clutched Ivy.

"This monstrous creature could rip a giant into tiny

pieces. His bite was deadly and he could kill without warning. The townspeople tried in vain to capture and kill the monster, but he returned, full moon after full moon. The creature couldn't be taken down with a gunshot or the threat of fire but instead vanished into the woods."

Nash paused. "The townspeople often awoke to find their cattle missing, or in some cases dismembered."

"Gross!" Ivy exclaimed.

Abby let out an audible gasp. "Tell us more!"

"It was only a matter of time, they feared, before the monster would be coming for them.

"The residents spent the nights of the full moon living in terror," he continued, "wondering what—or who—would be the beast's next victim."

"I can't take any more," Ivy said, covering her ears.

The darkness played with our imaginations. I spotted Dylan and Jake eyeing the woods as if every tree hid a stalking werewolf.

"Some dismissed the witnesses' accounts as drunken tall tales," Nash said. "Still others swore there was only one explanation . . ."

We waited in trembling awe.

"A citizen of Legend's Run had become a werewolf," he concluded in a serious tone.

His words left us silent.

Then he said with a deliberate voice, "But which of their neighbors had been overtaken by the glow of the full moon was never discovered."

"No—" Abby said.

"Still, generations later, underneath a full moon, the werewolf can be seen but has never been captured," Nash instructed. "By day he is an ordinary man, descended from that unlucky citizen of Legend's Run. But by night and under the curse of the moon, his eyes turn red, his muscles bulge, his teeth grow sharp, and he is covered with fur. A half man, half wolf who is tortured by his condition and threatening to anyone in his path."

Then he looked at each one of us. "Could the werewolf of Legend's Run have been one of your ancestors?" he wondered out loud.

The firelight cast ominous shadows against Nash's face, distorting his normally perfect features. His nose seemed as long as a warlock's, his ears pointy, his hair savagely spiky. His hazel eyes appeared fiery red.

He glared at us again. "Which one of us could be the Legend's Run werewolf's descendant?"

"Not me!" Abby blurted out.

Just then a gruesome howl was heard off in the distance.

Startled, I squeezed Ivy's hand. She let out a scream.

"Nash! You're scaring us!" Ivy charged.

"He's just fooling around," Jake assured.

Even Nash appeared startled. His eyes darted away from us. We heard the wailing again.

"I guess that could be your mom?" Dylan joked.

But Nash wasn't laughing.

Wolves weren't prone to approaching people or populated campsites, but it was dark, we had food, and we were closer to their homes than ours. I didn't want us to be the ones who proved the naturalists wrong.

"Don't worry, the fire will keep them away," Jake said.

"But our food won't," Abby said.

She was right. We had half-eaten s'mores, potato chips, and popcorn. It wasn't a good idea to possess food when hungry animals were in the vicinity.

"Toss everything into the fire," Jake commanded.

We quickly threw our remaining snacks into the flames, hoping to throw off the scent.

Ivy, Abby, and I glanced around us. All we could see was darkness and the formidable, looming trees.

When we turned back, Nash was gone.

"Nash?" I called.

There was no answer.

"Quit kidding!" Abby said.

"He's trying to prank us," Jake said. "I told you."

"Nash?" Ivy called.

The howling grew louder.

"This isn't funny, Nash!" Ivy said, her voice quivering.

"We'd better get to the cars," Abby said.

"And leave him here?" I asked.

"We don't even know where he is," Ivy said.

"What if something happened to him?" I wondered.

"We can't leave."

"We are better off getting our cars and going for help," Dylan said.

How could we abandon Nash? What if he was hurt? What if he was lost?

Dylan and Jake extinguished the fire with the surrounding dirt. We stood in total darkness. Just then we heard a howl again.

"Celeste, we have to go," Jake said.

"You said it yourself," I began. "It could be a prank."

"Then where is his video camera?" Abby said.

Dylan turned his flashlight on and pointed the beam around the area. We couldn't see anything but trees.

Jake pulled out his cell phone and called Nash. We waited for the sound of ringing, but all we heard was another howl.

"It went to voice mail," Jake finally said.

We hurried through the forest path, our flashlights illuminating the way.

The farther away from our campfire we were, the more nervous I became. I was upset to leave Nash behind.

"What if it's true?" Abby said. "What if a werewolf got him and now he's coming for us?"

We ran as fast as we could over dirt, roots, and fallen leaves. We finally reached the entrance to the woods where our cars were parked.

A figure was sitting inside Nash's car. We paused. We crept toward the car, Dylan and Jake leading the way.

The door opened and out popped Nash. I had to admit I was relieved, until he displayed a cheesy smirk.

The group laughed at his joke, now comforted that we'd found our friend. Jake high-fived him. But I wasn't so proud. I noticed beads of sweat dotting his brow. He appeared shaky.

Dylan wasn't as quick to give Nash props, either. "Hey, you left two guys alone in the woods with three girls. I think the joke's on *you*."

"Not so fast . . ." Nash took my hand, protecting his turf. "It was just a prank."

But I knew better.

We all hugged good-bye, and each couple got into their separate vehicles.

As Nash turned on the ignition of his car, his hands were still shaking. Nash had frightened himself—by his own story and by the timely howling animal. I slunk into the passenger seat and put on a brave face to mask my disappointment in my boyfriend's cowardice.

"You really had them fooled," I said flatly. "More so than you think."

TWO

legend's run

I'd lived my seventeen years in Legend's Run in an average American four-bedroom house with my "still married" parents and snotty older sister, Juliette. I had a decent upbringing in Legend's Run and didn't have too many complaints about the town except that it was full of social tension from being divided into two parts—the affluent suburbs on the east side and the blue-collar, rural town on the west. The Eastside was built up with new developments and rolling estates, while the Westside, or Riverside, was more agricultural. The Eastsiders felt their new homes were superior to the country homes, and the Riversiders resented that cornfields and silos were giving way to concrete driveways and street lamps. Each community had its own elementary schools, but all the students were combined at middle school. In high school, each side was reluctant to mix with the other out of pride, ignorance, or habit. The two sides were labeled by opposing student groups as either "snobs" or "hicks," though the truth was that neither label was entirely accurate. I smiled at everyone because it was the right thing to do. In addition, I always believed it took more energy for the two sides to stay apart than it would for them to finally come together.

Ivy Hamilton had been my closest friend since elementary school and lived in an adjacent subdivision in an estate home twice the size of mine.

It was my first day of first grade when a blond girl with a pale blue polka-dotted ribbon headband boarded the bus. I was sitting alone, watching the houses go by and wondering who lived in them, and inventing stories of their grand lives. Juliette had refused to sit with me and instead giggled with her friends a few rows back. The blond girl wore a tiny blue dress and matching sweater and a sparkling pink bracelet. The night before, my mom had brushed my tangled hair. I think I still had puffy eyes from all my bawling. I'm not sure what I wore, but I know it wasn't something that was "dry-clean only."

She was the only girl that day to wear a dress. She walked down the aisle of the bus like a contestant in a beauty pageant. I noticed the girl glaring at the boys and other girls. The boys were too shy to have her sit with them, while the girls were too jealous.

I was worried she would have to stand the whole way. When she reached me, I scooted over and smiled. Her glare turned into a big grin, accentuated by two dimples. She sat down beside me. She told me her name was Ivy and said I should get a dress just like hers so we could be twins. Even then I knew my mom wouldn't buy me a million-dollar outfit. When it was time to board the bus back home, Ivy saved a seat for me. She gave me her pink sparkly bangle bracelet. When I said I couldn't accept her gift, she insisted I take it. "I have five others at home," she said. I still have the outgrown tiny bangle in my jewelry box.

As we grew up, Ivy was interested in the ABC's—accessories, boys, and credit cards. She continued to be obsessed with fashion just as she was the first day we met. While she modeled clothes in dressing-room three-way mirrors for her mom, I sat cross-legged on the store bench doodling in my journal. I spent more time daydreaming and picturing myself in designer jeans than buying them.

In the eighth grade, Abby Kensington moved next door, or as I like to say, "next acre," to Ivy.

Ivy and I were swimming in her in-ground pool when a moving truck pulled in next door. A girl with a dark ponytail hopped out of the car. When she saw us, without hesitation she came right up and said, "Hi, I'm Abby Kensington. I know we'll be great friends."

I thought it was odd, since she didn't know a thing about Ivy or me. But it turned out Abby was right. She inserted herself into our twosome and we became an inseparable threesome.

Abby was athletic, with olive skin and black hair that waved like the sea, while Ivy was wiry and had alabaster skin and blade-straight blond hair. I fall somewhere in the middle.

At first, I was jealous of the new girl. Since Abby moved next door to Ivy, I was convinced they'd hang out together behind my back. They also shared a passion for designer clothes that I lacked. Abby was just as interested in scoring pristine high-end sports gear as she was winning a game. But Ivy never let anything sever our relationship.

Another attribute that my friends shared was accusing me of being too nice because I was cordial to everyone. Just because students were from various parts of the community didn't make us that different, I tried to tell them. We are all united by the same town and the same school, I reasoned, but Ivy and Abby preferred to hang out with Eastsiders. I tell them they aren't outright snobs but, rather, inward.

Juliette was of the same snooty mold. Two years older than me, she was cover-girl pretty. I was always in her shadow. Juliette did her best to make me a miniversion of herself, but it just didn't take. She took modeling classes, and as much as I tried to follow in her footsteps, I couldn't walk in a straight line even without a stack of books on my head.

While I ran around with Ivy and Abby, Juliette always kept company with one of the many adoring guys pursuing her.

Now that Juliette was a freshman in college, I was the only young adult in the house. I received more attention from my parents than normal and the house was much quieter with her absence, but I secretly did miss her. She didn't seem to miss home, though, since she was super busy dating college guys with Greek letters on their sweatshirts.

Unfortunately, my love life wasn't as glamorous as my sister's, until one day when I was approached by a guy I had had a crush on since first grade—Nash Hamilton.

Nash, Dylan, and Jake have had consecutive numbers on their football jerseys for as long as I can remember. Ivy and Abby had been dating Jake and Dylan since ninth grade. Since the three of them were best friends and two of them dated my best friends, it was always assumed that Nash and I should be sweethearts. But Nash always had a girlfriend.

It was at the end of sophomore year when Nash broke up with Heidi Rosen.

Ivy, Abby, and I were at a football practice when the team had a break. My friends chatted with their boyfriends, and I was writing ideas for future stories in my notebook. I went to the water fountain, and Nash approached me.

He leaned toward me and asked me out. I thought I didn't hear him correctly. When he repeated his request for a date, I almost laughed.

"No," I said, and walked away.

"Hey, come back."

It was then, I think, he really noticed me. Not as one of the popular girls, but as someone who was different. I don't think a girl had ever said no to him before. And I know he never chased after one.

I really thought it was a joke. Nash was known for pranks around school—gum on chairs, funny sayings on blackboards, sticking naughty pictures in textbooks—and I'd yet to be picked as his victim. I was sure that at any moment the school photographer was going to jump out from the bleachers and claim he'd captured the whole thing on video.

But more than that, I wondered why a hotshot like him would want to go out with me.

Ivy and Abby hung by the bleachers with a "What are you doing?" look on their faces.

I realized, then, that Nash wasn't kidding. It wasn't a prank, a hoax, or a hazing. Nash Hamilton was really asking me out.

Nash was a great catch—literally. He was the star running back on the football team.

I stopped in my tracks, and he came over to me with a surprised expression.

"Where are you running off to?" he asked.

"Uh . . . to look at my calendar," I said flippantly.

A smile crept across his face. He knew he'd met a challenge as big as competing against a 10-and-0 team.

"I may already have commitments," I said.

"What could be more important than a date with me?" he said seductively.

It was hard to resist him. He was very charming and charismatic. I did my best not to fold or quickly kiss up to him.

"I can think of a few things, but not many," I teased.

"Volunteering at a nursing home?" he wondered. "I've heard you are quite the humanitarian."

I wasn't sure if he was being sarcastic or sincere.

"In fact, yes," I said defiantly, and continued on.

"Hey, wait a minute," he said, stopping in front of me. "Then what about Saturday?"

I liked his tenacity, but I'd have been a fool to keep pushing him away.

"I'll cancel my plans," I said, knowing I wasn't busy.

"Good," he finally said. "Then mark my name in bold letters for Saturday night."

My stomach filled with butterflies. I caught up to my friends, who cheered and jumped higher than two caffeinated cheerleaders. Not only were we a threesome, we could be a sixsome.

I was as stunned as I was excited.

My sister was the one who always had the doorbell ringing for her. Now it was finally my turn.

Nash and I spent our first date at one of his football practices. My friends and I watched from the bleachers as the jocks did push-ups and sprints and caught passes. It wasn't as intimate and "get to know you" as I thought a first date would be. Since then, most of our dates had been spent with me on the sidelines, except for the occasional times he drove me home.

While I spent the games jotting down ideas for stories I

hoped to write, Ivy primped for Jake, and Abby jumped on the bleachers cheering for Dylan.

For some reason—or many—Nash and I didn't click together as easily as our counterparts. But I enjoyed the time we did share together. At day's end, though, when I shut down my computer, I often gazed out my bedroom window and up at the moon and wondered if, like my friends, I'd ever find true love.

THREE

the new guy in town

When a new student first arrived at Legend's Run High, their entrance didn't go unnoticed. Though everyone at Legend's Run High didn't hang out together, we all knew one another. It was odd to see a strange face.

It was late October, just after the campfire and werewolf-scare outing, and I was taking notes in government class when something caught my attention. Outside our classroom window, I saw an olive green beat-up Jeep pulling into an empty space in the student parking lot. I had to squint but noticed a WWF sticker on the front bumper. The driver-side door opened and a guy got out, wearing a vintage brown leather motorcycle jacket, torn jeans, and black hiking boots. He walked into the school building. A few moments later, the bell rang to change classes.

When I arrived at English class, I found my desk occupied. The guy in the vintage leather jacket was riffling through his backpack and placing a notebook on my desktop. In Mrs. Clark's class the students weren't seated in alphabetical order, or any other order for that matter, but rather we elected to take a desk where we wanted. Since school began, I sat in row six, first chair from the window. Abby sat next to me and Ivy next to her. Their boyfriends and Nash sat along the row nearest to the door.

When I noticed the stranger sitting in my seat, I didn't know what to do. I preferred to sit by my friends, but he was a new student and I wasn't about to tell him to move—I just didn't think it was polite. Instead, I chose an empty chair in the back.

Ivy spotted the stranger sitting in my seat and took it upon herself to confront the situation.

"That's okay—" I tried to say, but my words weren't heard.

"Excuse me, that desk is already taken," she said abrasively. Ivy got very territorial when it came to breaking up our clique. But it was okay with me. I could survive a day sitting on my own.

The new guy opened his notebook and looked up at the blond girl hovering over him, scolding him as if she were the teacher. I was hoping Ivy wasn't going to make a fuss. The new student would probably have moved had she been polite, but it seemed as if it was too late.

I hid behind my textbook. For a moment Ivy wasn't as confident as she was when she first approached him. I hoped this meant she was going to soften and either apologize or just return to her seat.

Instead, Abby joined her. Even though Ivy and Abby were pretty, their temperaments could sometimes leave even the kindest gentlemen challenging them to a duel rather than tipping their hats. Ivy threw her hair back and straightened her stance.

"This is my friend's desk," Ivy said, again in a very unpleasant tone. "She sits here every day."

The new guy didn't budge. He paused, weighing his words. "Are you two on the welcoming committee?" he asked. "I didn't see your pictures in the brochure."

A few skater students around him snickered. I couldn't help but giggle, too.

Abby tightened her lips. After all, she was used to competition, and it appeared that she wanted to win this battle.

"I understand you are new . . ." Abby charged, in a strong whisper, "but things work a certain way here, and the sooner you know this the easier it will be for you."

He sat up and leaned into Ivy. "This is your friend?" he said to her. "You might want to reconsider."

We all laughed again, even Dylan and Jake, who probably wished they could have said it. Abby and Ivy both folded their arms. It was clear the new student wasn't going to budge under the pressure of his two bossy classmates.

"No, *that* is our friend," they said in unison. Then they both pointed to me.

The new guy turned around. He was completely captivating and model gorgeous. His short hair was dark and wavy, his face as perfectly sculpted as I'd ever seen. He stared straight at me—his eyes a deep, riveting royal blue. We locked gazes and I almost lost my breath. My face flushed red. I was unable to look away, and I didn't really want to.

I'd never felt such a powerful stare—or witnessed such a handsome student.

He almost broke a smile, and my heart along with it.

The new student turned back, grabbed his notebook and backpack, and rose. He towered over my friends, who were blocking his way. They stepped aside, and he moved to an empty chair in the back of the class without another word.

As Ivy and Abby waved me over, I slunk back to my desk. When Mrs. Clark introduced the new student as Brandon Maddox, I wasn't about to turn around and make eye contact with him again.

Legend's Run High School's lunchroom was a microcosm of Legend's Run itself. Students stuck to their sides and, like religious sects, were subdivided. The usual gamers, jocks, skaters, and preps each had their own table.

Lunch, for me, was the highlight of the school day. I got to hang out with my friends and talk and eat—two of my favorite things.

When I reached the cafeteria, Ivy pulled Abby and me over to the vending machine.

"I finally have the four-one-one on the new guy," she began. "I heard he's a Westsider."

"Obviously," Abby said. "Did you see his coat?"

"There was nothing wrong with his coat. I liked it—" I tried. "Besides, you didn't have to—"

"Do you two want to hear this or not?" Ivy asked.

"Of course we do," Abby replied.

"He lives with his grandparents," Ivy began. "I think he's from Miller's Glen and was kicked out of his home. He's a juvie—"

"I heard he's a runaway," Abby said, placing a dollar into the machine.

"You did?" Ivy felt challenged that she wasn't on top of the breaking news story.

"Yes. A runaway," Abby said. She pushed a cola button and grabbed her diet soda.

"I heard he's a juvie," Ivy argued.

"I heard he's a runaway," Abby insisted.

"I heard . . ." I started.

"Yes?" they asked curiously.

"I heard that he's . . ."

"Go on . . ." they pried.

"I heard that he's a . . . *werewolf*!"

They both were aghast. "You did not!"

"That can't be true," Abby said. "I didn't hear that."

"Who told you that?" Ivy pressed.

I snickered. "Hello, are you kidding?"

Then we all broke out in laughter.

As we continued to crack up, I spotted Brandon sitting at a back table in the corner, alone. He was eating a sandwich and reading a book. The tables around him were filled, crowded with students gabbing and letting loose on their lunch break. This might have been my favorite part of the day, but for him, it must have been the most lonesome. My giggling subsided. I felt a huge ache in the pit of my stomach. It must be horribly lonely and difficult to come to a new school with no real friends—especially a school as cliquey as ours. And I felt ashamed that my two friends had been so unwelcoming.

I thought about going over to him and apologizing for my friends' behavior when two strong arms wrapped around my waist.

Suddenly I was lifted off the ground and swung around. I noticed a familiar class ring.

"Nash! Get off," I cried.

"What are you staring at?" he questioned, letting me down. "You should be staring at me."

He spun me so I faced him and he kissed me. Nash was a great kisser; for a brief moment I forgot where I was. But then it dawned on me. I wasn't in the privacy of a moonlit good-night kiss, but rather I was in the middle of the lunchroom with two hundred hungry gawkers.

I was never comfortable with Nash's public displays of

affection. It always felt as if he was only being demonstrative to prove his bravado to the student body rather than showing the unbridled passion of an amorous boyfriend.

He released me. I was dizzy—not so much from the kiss but from his spinning me. When my double vision returned to normal, I realized I was staring right across the lunchroom at Brandon. I sensed he'd been watching me the whole time.

There was something riveting about him, unusual, and different. I wasn't sure why I felt embarrassed in front of Brandon more so than the other students watching us. All I knew was that I did. I wiped my mouth with my sleeve, sat down at our table with my back toward the new student, and distracted myself with a low-carb lunch and wonderfully inane conversation.

FOUR

walking with a werewolf

Pine Tree Village Retirement Community was a non-descript two-story brown brick building that could have doubled for an apartment building. It included assisted living, independent units, and a full nursing wing and was about ten minutes north from my house.

I enjoyed volunteering at the nursing home. If I had a dismal day at school or was struggling with Nash, I forgot my worries. These seniors were very different from the seniors at my school. Most of the residents were happy to see a fresh, young face. And even though many of them told me the same story over and over, it was interesting to hear the tales of past generations in Legend's Run or cities and countries I'd never visited.

Abby and Ivy, convinced wrinkles were contagious,

refused to set foot in the senior community, and Nash was always too busy, practicing, playing, or preparing for sports. I knew it was unlikely he'd come to visit other people's grand-parents. That didn't make my friends bad, but it would have been cool if I could have shared the experience with them. It was something I'd always done on my own.

Mr. Worthington was my favorite resident at Pine Tree Village. For a gentleman who was eighty-nine years old, he was quite cute. Mr. Worthington was alert, mobile, and in shape. We walked the hallways or outside commons areas together. He always dressed in khaki pants and a cardigan sweater and kept his fuzzy white hair neatly combed.

Every time I visited Pine Tree Village, I was always greeted by the receptionist, who had me sign in and pointed me to an area where the staff could use an extra hand. Today's visit was extra special. It was Halloween and I'd dressed as Little Red Riding Hood. I wore a red hoodie, the arms loosely tied around my neck and the body as a cape, along with a black bodice, white T-shirt, and red flippy skirt. I finished off my fairy-tale look with white folded socks and a pair of Juliette's black pumps she'd left behind in her closet. It wasn't a good idea to pass out candy to the residents, so I came with "Happy Halloween" pins I'd made instead. I grabbed a small basket my mom used for magazines and stuck a loaf of bread in it.

The normally hospital white lobby was decorated with black and orange streamers, cotton-candy-like spiderwebs, and ghost, mummy, and black-cat die cuts. A sign posted in the lobby read: HALLOWEEN DANCE AT 7 P.M.

I teetered over to the reception desk, where I was welcomed by a very friendly witch.

"You look great," Sally said through blackened-out teeth. I could barely hold my laughter inside as the straitlaced receptionist offered me a tray of pumpkin cookies.

"I'll grab one on the way out," I said.

"Little Red," I heard a man's voice call.

I didn't even respond to my new name until I heard it called again.

"Little Red, over here."

An elderly man wearing werewolf fangs, a brown-tipped nose, and a fluffy brown wig was standing a few yards away in the lobby next to a grand piano. I almost didn't recognize Mr. Worthington at first, but his brown cardigan sweater and khaki pants gave him away.

"Happy Halloween," I said, handing him a button.

"It's Halloween?" he asked. "No one told me."

I laughed at the elderly werewolf. I really adored Mr. Worthington. His youthful spirit was like a chandelier illuminating a darkened room.

"Let me help you," I said, pinning the button on his sweater. "I'm not sure I should be seen with a wolf, much less a werewolf. The residents will think we planned this."

"Let them think what they want," he said. "I've never seen a prettier girl in red."

I blushed to match the color of my hoodie.

"Well, I've never seen such a kind-looking werewolf," I commented back.

"So you've seen one?" he asked seriously.

"The closest thing I've seen to a werewolf was when my sister, Juliette, tried to perm her own hair."

Nurse Bridget, the head nurse on the first floor, walked by. Overhearing the final part of our conversation, she stepped over.

"Charlie, are you going on about werewolves again?" she asked, putting her arm around him. "You don't want to frighten Celeste away. She's our only steady volunteer."

"I haven't said a word. No one wants to listen to an old man, anyway."

"That's okay," I assured Nurse Bridget. "I promise I won't be too frightened."

"Every Halloween," she said, "Charlie tells us about the Legend's Run werewolf. Someone says they saw something furry in the woods years ago and people can't stop talking about it. It's like the Loch Ness Monster. A big hoax."

"My boyfriend was just telling my friends and me about that recently."

"So you already know?" Mr. Worthington asked.

"I guess as much as anyone else knows. But I'd love to hear about it from you."

Mr. Worthington brightened, knowing he finally had a captive audience.

"Celeste," Nurse Bridget said in an apologetic tone, "I'd

love it if you could visit with some of the other residents. I'm sure they would be delighted. Mr. Worthington, can you tell her the story later?"

"Of course," Mr. Worthington said. "It's one thing I never forget. Now, where I left my glasses—*that* I can't remember."

"I won't be long," I said. I didn't want to abandon Mr. Worthington, but I had a number of pins I had to pass out and was more worried about upsetting Nurse Bridget.

I pinned, hugged, and took pictures with as many residents as I could find.

When I returned to the lobby, I found the elderly werewolf sleeping on a sofa. I was tempted to sit down and take off my painful pumps, since I was exhausted, but I knew I'd have as difficult a time getting up as he would.

I grabbed a small blanket from an adjacent chair and placed it on his lap.

"Is it time for dinner?" he asked, suddenly stirring.

"Yes, and it's time for me to go—"

"So soon?"

"I'm sorry it took so long," I said. "But I can walk you to the dining room."

"What did I do to deserve such a beautiful escort?" he asked kindly.

"You were going to tell me your story," I replied eagerly.

"Oh yes. You remind me of my wife when she was very young. We met here in Legend's Run."

I nodded. I'd heard that story many times but tried to pay attention as if I were listening to it for the first time.

"When we were young, Legend's Run was still a farming and mill town along the river. Not like now, where custom homes dot the landscape.

"But in the last fifty years the mill closed and people moved away from the town and came from the neighboring cities and developed the eastern side of Legend's Run. The Westside farmers continue to maintain their land. The east side became too congested and Riverside's commercial property too vacant. We moved away to New York, and eventually the rest of the Worthington family moved on, too."

My eyes had half glazed over and I tried my best to listen, as I'd heard this story countless times. "Did you miss it here?" I asked when he paused.

"Yes. And so did my wife. I promised her we'd return to Legend's Run to ride out our years that remained. I am a man of my word," he said with a grin.

There was one story I hadn't heard from Mr. Worthington. "And the werewolf? Did he live on the Westside or the East?"

The elderly man perked up even more. He was poised to tell his tale.

"The creature calls the woods his home. Where he can hide from curious people and most importantly from the threat of the full moon. Since the moon can appear to us as full for several days, it makes the werewolf that much more tormented. It was many years ago when he was first spotted in one of the tree-filled areas along Riverside," he whispered. "But you must never go in the woods alone, a girl like you."

We reached the dining room, and a staff member approached Mr. Worthington.

The dining room was full of residents and staff wearing my handmade pins.

"It's the Legend's Run werewolf," the aide announced. Several residents clapped.

I watched as the elderly resident was treated by his peers as if he were a celebrity.

"Please remind him to remove those fangs before he eats," I said to the aide as I made a weary exit.

That night Ivy hosted a Halloween party at her über-house—five bedrooms, a three-car garage, and a basement that could entertain our entire school.

Ivy opened the door dressed like a runway model, in a black-and-white minidress and white patent-leather go-go boots. Abby stood next to her brandishing a big smile, two pigtails, and a borrowed cheerleading uniform—complete with an "LR" letter and spirit buttons. I felt worse for the wear in my homemade costume.

"I want to go back and change," I said, still standing on the stoop.

"What gives?" Ivy said. "You look so cute!"

"I . . ."

"Get in here," Ivy said.

"No, I think I'd feel better if I changed into something else."

"Your outfit is ten times more creative than ours," Abby said.

"But—"

"No buts! Just get yours in here." She took my wrist and dragged me inside.

There were already a few of our classmates milling about her home, trying to talk over the pounding music.

"Have the guys arrived?" I asked.

"Not yet, but I can't wait until they do. I'm sure their costumes will be killer."

"How was Pine Tree?" Abby asked. "I bet one of those old men might leave you something when . . ."

"That's morbid—" Ivy said. "That's not why Celeste volunteers there."

"I know," Abby said, "but it could be one of the perks."

Just then the front door burst open and we could hear Jake and Dylan's voices.

"They're here!" Ivy called. My friends eagerly headed for the door, swishing their miniskirts, and I followed, trying not to scrape my heels on her pristine hardwood floors.

Dylan raced around the grand entryway, dressed as Superman. He picked up Abby and she squealed as he pretended to save her.

"And look at your hot outfit!" Jake said with a twang. He

had a piece of straw in his mouth, carried a stuffed cow, and was barefoot.

Ivy appeared disappointed and confused.

"What are you?" she asked.

"Duh, I'm a Westsider," he proclaimed.

I rolled my eyes.

"You're so ignorant," Ivy whispered, half horrified. "You're going to embarrass me at my party."

"Have you been to the Westside?" he asked.

"I know they wear shoes," I said, shaking my head.

I looked to Ivy for help.

She reached into my purse and pulled out my eyeliner. She grabbed Jake's chin with one hand and with the other drew several circles on his face and quickly colored them in.

"What are you doing?" Jake asked, annoyed.

"Now you are as you should be," Ivy announced. "A cow!"

Everyone laughed—except, of course, for Jake.

"Where is Nash?" I asked, anxious to find him. I was looking forward to seeing what he wore.

"Parking the car," Dylan said.

I imagined at any minute Nash would be running into the house dressed as a superhero, swooping me up in his arms and carrying me off to safety, or a knight taking me as his princess and challenging any guest who vied for my attention to a duel, or even a rock star who'd get down on one knee and serenade me with a love song.

Instead, Nash entered Ivy's foyer as he always did—in jeans and a long-sleeved polo.

"What are you?" I asked.

He checked me out—eyeing my short skirt, bare legs, and high heels.

"I guess I'm the Big Bad Wolf!" Nash said as he grabbed me around the waist and pulled me to him. "Grr," he said with a growl.

The partygoers around us broke out in laughter, as if Nash were a headlining comedian. But I didn't think his joke was funny.

I felt awkward and even let down, but I didn't want my true feelings to spoil the party. I did my best to disguise my disappointment by making myself busy and handing out drinks in Ivy's airplane-hangar-size kitchen.

I watched as Abby and Ivy talked, giggled, and snuggled with their boyfriends. I was excited and flushed and giddy many times when I was with Nash, but I felt something was lacking that my friends had.

"What's with you?" Nash asked. "You seem aloof."

"I'm not, I'm just helping Ivy out," I said.

"Ivy's making out with Jake. The only thing you can be helping her out with now is giving her an oxygen tank."

It was odd; Nash and I seemed to sense each other's feelings when those around us weren't as in tune.

I was attempting to refill the ice when he took the silver monogrammed bucket from me.

"What's up, Parker?"

"Nothing," I said with a forced smile.

"You're mad that I didn't come in costume?" he asked.

"I'm not mad . . ."

"But disappointed."

I shrugged my shoulders.

"I didn't know it meant that much to you," he said.

I gazed down at my shoes.

He took my chin and raised it so I was facing him.

"I guess I should have . . . it just seems so silly," he said. He glanced at the crowd, then back at me. "I don't want to wear a clown wig or Darth Vader mask. You'd think I'd look ridiculous."

"You're afraid of what I'd think?" I asked, surprised.

"I guess. You and everyone else."

"Nash, you are gorgeous," I said. "No matter what you wore, no one would be laughing *at* you."

It was funny to me that deep down inside, the all-star athlete of Legend's Run High still was insecure.

"Are you just charming me?" I asked.

"Did it work?" he wondered aloud.

I couldn't help but smile.

But before I knew it, Nash kissed me and I was quickly lost in his lips. At that moment I no longer cared how he was dressed.

FIVE

love and the library

It was mid-November, and a few weeks had passed since my friends and I were circled around a campfire in the woods and Nash had told us his frightening werewolf story. Footballs, goalposts, and grass were replaced with basketballs, hoops, and hardwood floors. The red, gold, and orange autumn leaves had fallen or been blown away and now many trees stood naked. The temperatures fell, too. There was just a dusting of snow on the ground.

I loved the first fresh snow when it blanketed the town and closed the schools, or a weekend snowfall when it accumulated enough for us to stay indoors with a cozy comforter, a good book, and tasty hot chocolate. I loved the sound of the snow crunching underneath my boots or the ultralight snowfall on a silent street. I loved magical moments when the only impressions in the snow were the tiny footprints of a bird. And I cherished the memories of when Juliette and I were younger and dragged our sleds to Hillside or another nearby slope.

We hadn't had a major snowfall yet, however, only cold weather and occasional flurries. Snow wasn't nearly as great when it wasn't enough to close school. Then it was just inconvenient and messy to trudge through, soaking the hallways, and leaving me crossing my frozen fingers that I wouldn't wipe out and land on my backside in front of the entire student body.

Abby, Ivy, their beaux, and Nash and I were in library study hall keeping warm. In our English class we were studying American folklore and had been assigned a paper on the subject. I kept thinking about Mr. Worthington's werewolf story. I decided werewolves would be a good subject for my essay. It was one thing to have Nash tell a campfire story to scare us, but I was even more intrigued that Mr. Worthington seemed impassioned by the tale himself. And besides, I could use him as a resource for my paper. Nash's story was exhilarating and frightening because of the thought a werewolf could be living among us. Though I didn't believe in their existence, I could only imagine that the early settlers had felt alone like we had been in the woods.

I went to the stacks, scanning the aisles for anything werewolf. I picked up several books. *The Encyclopedia of Monsters* and *Myths and Mysteries*. I found *The Book of Werewolves* and was pulling it off the shelf when it slipped from my hand.

As I bent down to pick it up, someone was already handing it to me. It was Brandon Maddox.

For the past few months I'd only had brief encounters with Brandon or passed him on the way to class. We were in a few classes together but he sat in the back, his head buried underneath his wavy locks. He always ate lunch by himself. I'd never admit to my friends that I thought Brandon was handsome. He had deep, royal blue eyes that shined through his short, shaggy dark hair. If he were an Eastsider, he'd surely be one of the most popular guys in school. But since fate led him to be on the Westside, he was greatly ignored.

Brandon didn't say anything. I sensed it was not because he was afraid to but because he was the kind of person who chose his words carefully.

I wanted to say thank you. But as he continued to gaze into my eyes, my words escaped me.

"Celeste! Get over here," Ivy called. "What are you doing?"

I headed over to my friends, feeling slightly more flushed than I had when I'd left them.

"Werewolves?" Nash asked when he saw me holding my stack of books.

"I thought I could ask you to tell the class the Legend's Run Werewolf legend. I could score some extra points," I said.

"Is this my paper or yours? I'm not working on two," he said, and buried his head in *Sports Illustrated*. "Besides, I was hoping to buy my paper off the internet."

"Nash!" I said, horrified by his plan.

"I'm just kidding, Parker," he said to me. "Lighten up."

"I'm considering quilting," Ivy said proudly.

"Quilting?" Jake asked.

"Yes, many people told stories through narrative quilting."

"Boring!"

"Of course it would be boring to *you*," Ivy said. "If it doesn't involve cheerleaders, you don't want to hear about it."

"Were there naked quilters?" Jake asked. "Now, that would be interesting!"

Ivy playfully hit her boyfriend.

"I was thinking of investigating witches," Abby proudly announced.

"You won't have to go far to investigate that," Dylan said.

"Well, thanks," Abby said sarcastically.

"No—I mean you can ask Dr. Meadows," he said.

"Who?" Ivy asked.

"That witch doctor in Riverside," Dylan replied. "My mom went there for acupuncture and said she sells books on everything. I'm sure she has information on witches."

Abby appeared skeptical.

"While you're there, maybe you can get your fortune told," Dylan continued. "See if I'm getting any action from you this weekend."

"You want *me* to go to the Westside and talk to a witch doctor?" Abby said. "Are you crazy?"

"Are you chicken?" Dylan challenged.

"Of course not!" Abby replied.

"Going to Riverside," he taunted. "Afraid you'll want to move in?"

"No. It's just I have volleyball practice." Abby wasn't one to be pushed around; she had her reputation to uphold.

"I dare you," Jake said.

"Dare?" Abby asked.

"Yes, dare!" he repeated.

"Fine," Abby said, shaking his hand. "Ivy, Celeste, and I will get our fortunes told by Dr. Meadows."

"I don't believe you," Dylan said. "You, in Riverside? I'm not sure they'll let you in."

"They better," she said. "And I'll prove it to you. I'll get a reading and then a receipt."

"Whatever you say," Dylan said with a laugh.

"And when I do," Abby continued, "you'll have to be our servants for a day."

"Aren't we already?" he asked.

"And if you don't, then you'll have to be ours." Jake smiled.

"I guarantee *that* won't be happening," I said.

My friends cuddled and studied with their boyfriends as I imagined what my fortune might be.

I gazed outside. I could see the moon hanging in the cloudless blue sky. It looked lonely, staring back at me. I wondered if it thought the same of me.

a penny for your thoughts

After school, Ivy, Abby, and I left the suburbs for the more rural side of Legend's Run. Farms, lakes, and vineyards filled the landscape. I always thought the Westside had more character. However, Ivy and Abby were only interested in the strip and indoor malls, restaurants, and fast food in the burbs. Even the yuppies didn't stop in Riverside but rather pedaled through it on the bike trail on weekend outings. As the years passed, I had no reason to venture there on my own.

As we came into Riverside, antiques shops, used car lots, and neighborhoods without homeowners associations lined the terrain. The businesses had left for the suburbs, and the downtown wasn't as viable as it once was. However, a small town remained, including a hardware store, bars, flea and farmers' markets, a biker bar, and Gerald's Garage—where Gerald still pumped the gas.

"Let's not run out of gas!" Ivy said.

"It's not like we're on the other side of the earth," I said. "We could walk back."

"Are you crazy? Walk?" Abby asked, horrified. This comment was coming from the jayvee champion track star. I guess it just mattered *where* she walked.

"Jake said it's dangerous down by Riverside. So far, it doesn't look that bad to me."

"I think it's beautiful," I said, gazing into a wooded area. "All these trees and hills."

"But where do people who live here shop?" Ivy asked. "I haven't seen a mall for miles."

"Yes," Abby said. "And where is a community pool? There aren't even any health clubs here."

"I guess you don't need a treadmill if you are plowing a field." Ivy laughed.

"They have cars, just like us," I defended. "If they want to go to a mall, they drive just like we do."

We continued on and passed a wooded area that ran along the road for about half a mile. Then we came into the small downtown area.

On the tiny main street many shops were vacant, but the ones that remained—a tattoo and piercing parlor, a hair salon, and a florist—seemed to be thriving.

"We could get a tat," Abby said. "I think a tramp stamp

would be really cool. Dylan would love it."

"No one is coming at me with a needle," Ivy said. "Not even for a guy."

I imagined the tattoos my friends would have: Ivy's would be a designer label drawn on her arm, and Abby might have one of a volleyball.

Ivy parked her car at the meter in front of Penny for Your Thoughts.

"I don't have change," Ivy said. Ivy was used to paying for things with plastic. I don't even think she owned a coin purse.

"How much should I put in?" Abby asked, rummaging through her purse.

"I don't know how long it takes to get a reading. I've never done it before," Ivy said. "Is it longer than a massage or a pedi?"

I shrugged my shoulders. I'd had a pedicure several years ago for my sister's graduation. I was so relaxed and zoned out I forgot how long it took.

I fished some change out of my hoodie pocket and fed the meter.

Penny for Your Thoughts was quite the curiosity shop. Candles, crystals, jewelry, books, and the smell of incense filled the one-room store.

I examined books on healing, numerology, astrology, angels, and interpreting dreams. There were so many different paranormal ideas, I wasn't sure how a person decided which one to believe in.

I did like the mood of the shop. It was very calm and relaxing. Soothing mandolin, harp, and flute music played over the sound of a roaring ocean. The store was a nice change of pace from our frenetic high school, with lockers slamming and students yelling across the hallway. I was just hoping I could stay awake long enough to get my fortune told.

"Doesn't anyone run this place?" Abby asked. She got irritated if she wasn't immediately greeted like a VIP upon entering a store or restaurant.

"If she was truly psychic, wouldn't she know we were here?" I whispered.

"Maybe she does and doesn't want to talk to us," Abby said pensively.

But I was suspicious. Maybe Dr. Meadows wasn't going to come out right away so she could overhear our discussions. Or maybe she was watching us on a hidden camera.

Abby perused books on witches, and Ivy headed straight for the jewelry displays. Any gift shop was a potential sale to her. She was sizing up some aquamarine earrings that matched her eyes. I thought they were beautiful, and if I had more money, I, too, would have loved a pair. I caressed the glassy stones, trying to figure out how long it would take for me to buy them. Ivy didn't even bat an eyelash.

"That's not why we are here," Abby said, taking the earrings from Ivy and returning them to the jewelry stand.

Abby rapidly tapped a bell on the counter.

"Maybe she's back there casting a spell or something," she said. "Or making potions."

No one came out to wait on us. We were certain the store was open but not sure how long we should stay. My friends were often impatient—but not this time.

"We can leave," I offered.

"Not without my receipt," Abby said. "If you think I'm going to be Dylan's servant for a week . . . I can only imagine the horrors he'll ask of me. Clean his locker? Forget it. Besides, I've been thinking all day of things I can have him do. I really could use a back massage."

"And Jake can return those skirts I bought at the mall," Ivy said.

I wondered what I'd ask Nash to do as my servant. Carry my books? My backpack worked fine. Do my homework? I wasn't a cheater. Clean my room? He never came over. Then it occurred to me. The one thing that would really make Nash squirm. I'd have him host a party and make him invite a Westsider.

"You're right," I said. "We need to get those receipts!"

Now I tapped the bell.

A woman appeared, startling all of us.

"I'm so sorry to keep you girls waiting. I hope you had a chance to look around. What brings you in today?"

"Are you Dr. Meadows?" Abby asked.

"Yes, have you heard of me?" she asked incredulously.

Dr. Meadows's appearance wasn't that of a typical doctor.

She didn't wear a lab coat or scrubs. She also didn't look like a witch doctor. She did, however, have long gray hair tied back in a ponytail, and she wore an oversized silk blouse, a floor-length scrunchie skirt, and layered beaded necklaces. I guessed she was in her fifties.

Dr. Meadows had a gentle energy around her. Not that I was an aura reader, but I imagined hers to be a mixture of warm and bright hues.

"We'd like our fortunes told," Abby said.

"You mean an interpretive reading?" she asked as if fortune-telling was so "yesterday." "Have you had one before?"

Again, I figured she should already know this, but I just shook my head.

Dr. Meadows turned the sign hanging on the door from OPEN to CLOSED.

"We can't have any distractions," she said. "Let's go into the reading room."

The reading room was painted indigo blue, with a hanging teardrop chandelier. There was a square table with chairs on each end. In the corner were a small waterfall and a tea service.

"I thought you'd have a spooky room with a crystal ball," Abby said.

I wouldn't admit it to Dr. Meadows, but I was surprised, too. Though I didn't subscribe to her New Age philosophy, I certainly respected that this was her establishment, not ours.

"I'll go first," I offered. I just wanted to get this over with.

"No—I will," Abby bulldozed, and scooted into the chair before I could land on it. Ivy and I took the empty chairs by the tea service and observed.

Dr. Meadows took Abby's hand and matched her gaze. Then the doctor closed her purple-painted eyelids. I imagined she was planning her dinner menu.

"You are a very spirited girl," she began. "That is good. It will take you far. But you can relax. It is okay to slow down. You have your whole life ahead of you."

"Wow—she's good," Abby said.

I wasn't impressed. Just by looking at Abby, a stranger could tell she was athletic and high-strung. And it wasn't much of a reading, I thought. Was she going to meet a handsome stranger? Was she going to win the grand prize on a reality show?

Ivy and Abby swapped chairs. Ivy's hand was ultra-feminine, as dainty as the porcelain teacup. Her perfectly manicured nails were without a hangnail or uneven polish like mine.

"Worldly things are very important to you," Dr. Meadows said. "But it is okay to find the things that matter most inside."

Ivy was very pleased with her reading. It was as if Dr. Meadows had been a mentor to her all of her life. And all she did was feed her a line from any self-help book.

Dr. Meadows offered us tea. "It's ginseng. Lots of anti-oxidants."

Ivy and Abby pounced on the idea of having a few drinks. We hadn't stopped at a coffee shop and I knew they were suffering from latte withdrawal.

"Do you have sugar?" Abby asked.

"It is supposed to be taken in its pure form," Dr. Meadows said, and poured two cups. Then she turned to me.

"No thank you," I politely said.

"Ah . . . a skeptic," Dr. Meadows said. "Always one in the room. Dragged here by your friends? It's okay," she offered again. "I didn't put anything into the tea."

I know. I watched you, I wanted to say.

Ivy and Abby were sipping from their teacups like we were dining with the queen of England.

Dr. Meadows held my hand for a moment. She was dead silent.

"I see snow," she began. "Beware of the woods . . . of the sounds of howling. There could be outsiders who will turn . . . underneath the glow of the full moon."

Chills raced up my arm and straight to the top of my neck. I tried to pull my hand away, but her grasp was too tight.

We struggled for a moment until finally she released her grip.

"I think it's time we go," I said, rising.

Dr. Meadows still seemed to be in a trance.

I turned to my friends, who reluctantly returned their

teacups to the table.

"We have to go . . ." Abby said.

"Yes?" Dr. Meadows said, coming back to life. She sighed an exhausted sigh.

I marched out of the room, and Ivy and Abby followed.

Abby grabbed a benign, humorous book on witchcraft for her essay and she and I placed our money on the counter when Dr. Meadows finally appeared. Ivy handed her a credit card.

"We need three receipts, please," Abby requested.

Dr. Meadows handed us our change and gave Ivy her receipt to sign.

"I hope you will come again," Dr. Meadows said, escorting us to the door. "At least for some tea."

"This is the best time we've ever had!" Abby squealed, giving Dr. Meadows a hug.

"I'm coming here for jewelry!" Ivy said.

I, on the other hand, decided this would be my last trip to Penny for Your Thoughts. I would have gladly traded in my bogus reading for the stunning, luminous earrings, since they wound up being the same price. Now I knew why they called them "fortunes."

When we reached the door, Dr. Meadows had parting words for my friends. "Thank you so much for coming," she said, giving each an embrace. "You're such delightful girls. Remember what is inside of you—not just what is on the outside."

My beaming friends exited the shop.

Then, suddenly, Dr. Meadows turned to me and grasped my shoulder.

"Celeste," she said vehemently. "Beware of a kiss under the full moon. It will change your life forever."

east meets west

Dr. Meadows's words haunted me. Her messages to me were so specific yet, at the same time, mysterious. My reading had not been anything like my friends'. It wasn't about my personality but rather about events. The snow. The woods. Howling. The moon. A kiss? Not only did I get a crazy fortune, but I'd blown my allowance for the entire week on foolishness.

As we dished by the car, Abby and Ivy cracked up.

"I thought she was great!" Ivy said. "She was so right on with me."

"Well, it wasn't hard to figure out that you are athletic," I said to Abby. "And that you are a fashion diva," I stated to Ivy.

"Then how do you explain yours?" Ivy asked.

"Hocus-pocus," I said. "She had to throw in something to get our money's worth."

"I can't wait to tell Nash what she said," Ivy said. "He better stay away from you and the woods."

"Oh, great—I'm going to be late to volleyball practice," Abby said, checking her phone. "If I'm late, I'll have to do extra laps."

Ivy didn't have time to drop me off. Instead she would have to take us all back to school. I wanted some downtime and wasn't in the mood to travel back to Legend's Run High.

"Are you sure?" Ivy asked when I announced I was going to walk home along the bike trail.

"It's just up the road. I can almost see my house from here," I reassured them. My home was less than a mile away, and I thought the cool air in my lungs would perk me up.

"I don't want you walking home alone," Ivy said. "Please come with us."

"We don't have much time to argue," Abby urged. "She'll be fine. Her house isn't *that* far away."

I nodded in agreement.

As my friends departed, I followed a bike trail that ran between the Westside woods and the main road. As long as I stayed on the path, I'd be home within twenty minutes. I began walking, enjoying the sights of endless trees, the smell of November air, and the sounds of geese flying overhead. Birds' nests high atop a few of the naked trees were clearly visible. I took out my binder and jotted down a few notes, wanting to remember these elements for future stories. What I didn't anticipate was the snow.

It began with a few flakes. Tiny frosted crystals started to sprinkle down, tapping my fur-lined boots and knit gloves. I was delighted; it made my rural journey that much more enchanting. I loved fresh snow, gentle and whimsical, coloring the sky and trees bright white. The flakes hit my worn binder, dampening my pages, so I stopped and placed it in my backpack. I held out my hand and captured a few flakes in my glove. They didn't dissolve right away; I could see the tiny, intricate crystal formations. I didn't remember a snowfall forecast and assumed it would be a light sprinkling for the next few minutes and enjoyed the tapping of snowflakes against my cheeks.

As I continued on, the falling flakes grew bigger, dotting the road and grass. The wind picked up and the now quarter-size flakes flew into my hair and face, tickling me. I covered my head with my fleece hood. The wintry scene was beautiful; I could have walked in these conditions for days. But it wasn't long before the wind blew with huge gusts. I zipped up my hoodie and walked on. The snow increased and pelted down while the wind picked up speed.

Instead of the elements painting a blissful picture, they began to fight against me. It was more difficult to view the trees in the distance, and I was annoyed that it was growing colder and getting harder to walk. Within a few minutes, the road was caked with snow. The sky was completely overcast—gray-and-white clouds engulfed it. The trees I could easily make out a few minutes ago were now difficult to see. I realized if I couldn't see anything, then an approaching driver's vision would be impaired, too. There wasn't much room between the road and the bike trail, and I worried a driver might drift off the road now that the lines were invisible. To play it safe, I stepped off the bike path and caught my breath by a row of evergreens. The tall, lush trees blocked most of the wind and snow. The scene around me was breathtaking, but when the gusts grew even stronger and objects only a few yards away became invisible, I decided to press on. I hung on to several evergreens as I walked, using them to guide me forward. Before I knew it, I was grabbing brush instead. I could no longer see the trail or the road. I was frustrated. As the elements were battling against me, all I saw was snow above me, in front of me, and on either side. I could barely keep my eyes open. I was getting really cold and wanted to get home. I walked from tree to tree. I assumed they were paralleling the road and bike trail. I continued on until I grew tired. I stopped by an old oak and leaned against it, catching my breath again. I hadn't seen anything but trees for a while. Then I realized—where was I?

The snowfall was getting worse. I was frightened. I knew the Eastside very well and it was so developed that people, businesses, and homes were in easy reach. I decided to stay put for a few minutes and ride out the storm. When it was clear, I'd get my bearings back and figure out my location.

If Ivy and Abby could see me now, they'd surely freak. They'd blame themselves for not insisting I return with them and gripe at me for being so stubborn. One thing was for sure, they'd never let me set foot in Riverside again.

There were no signs of civilization—Gerald's Garage, or a cabin. I was really getting cold. My nose was starting to sting, and the freezing temperatures were penetrating my thin hoodie. Originally, I was only a short distance from my house, and now I'd managed to get myself so turned around, I wasn't even sure where I was on the planet. My good mood had soured. The weather had gotten the best of me. My chest felt heavy and my breathing became short. My heart pounded. And though I was cold, I started to perspire. I still had no idea where I was and which direction I'd been going. And most important, I didn't know how I was going to get out.

The wind and snow weren't ceasing; instead, the snow drove down in a blinding heavy fall, and the wind whipped it around me.

I decided to call my parents. I knew someone would surely come to my rescue. I pulled out my cell but couldn't get a signal.

I remembered that sinking feeling when I was a kid and I was lost in a store and feared my mom would leave me behind. And though I was older, I felt the same isolation and desperation. I took a deep breath, attempting to calm myself.

I tried my phone again, but still no connection.

I knew the world was bustling like it normally did in inclement weather. Children coming home from school grabbing their sleds. Adults stocking up on milk and bread at the grocery store. And then there was me—stuck in the middle of nowhere.

The solitude was eerie. It wasn't like when I was inside my bedroom listening to my music, knowing my family would return from a night out. There was no one coming for me. Ivy and Abby were heading in the opposite direction and wouldn't realize for hours that I wasn't home. Nash was at practice and wouldn't contact me until late evening. And my mom thought I was with Ivy and Abby. She wouldn't wonder where I was until dinner.

I should have been home by now. The sun would be setting soon and Mom would be serving a delicious, piping hot meal. Instead, I was growing hungry and was lost in the woods in a major blizzard. The snow began to rise around me. It was only going to get darker and colder.

If I wasn't in trouble now, I knew I would be by nightfall. I'd heard about the seriousness of frostbite and hypothermia. I imagined being forced to spend the night here, taking shelter by a tree. I couldn't imagine sleeping in the snow without a tent, a down sleeping bag, or a burning fire.

With no protection from the wind, snow, and cold, I was sure to freeze. Many creatures called the woods their home; I didn't know what they might do to a lost intruder.

Time seemed to slow down to a grinding halt. Every

minute felt like days. Had I been lost for a few moments or a few hours? The bright white sky grew darker. The sun had gone behind the storm clouds, and now I feared it was moments away from setting.

"Help!" I called. "Please—can anyone hear me?" I shouted as loudly as my voice would carry.

Snow tapped against my face and eyelashes and fell into my mouth. My calls went unanswered.

"Where am I?" I shouted. Frustrated, I kicked my boot into the snow. I felt like throwing my phone, too, but I knew it was my only lifeline—even if it didn't work. I clung to it, hoping once I changed positions it would catch a signal. I had to do something. Snow reflected off the clouds and illuminated part of the woods. I had to make a decision—continue on and hope I reached the road, or backtrack and retrace my footprints? I chose to attempt to try to return the way I came. I was following my wayward footsteps when I heard a cry in the distance. It was the howl of a wolf.

I froze.

I tried not to panic. For all I knew, the wolf was miles away. I recalled tanning in the summer's sun with my eyes closed and how voices always seemed much closer than the people talking actually were. This must be the same thing, I tried to assure myself.

The air was getting colder. I covered my mouth with my scarf to warm my face, breath, and lungs. The snow and wind continued to push against me but I knew I had to move. I took a few steps. It was as difficult as walking on the moon.

Then I heard the howl again. This time it was definitely closer, eyes open or not.

I started to walk, briskly this time. Though I was tired and my boots were now heavy, I ventured on. I had a fifty-fifty chance of going farther into the woods or making my way out of it. Normally I wasn't a gambling person, but I didn't have a choice. It was hunt or be hunted.

When the wolf cried again, I picked up my pace and moved quickly, running through my filling tracks. At this point I didn't care which way I was going, just as long as it was away from danger.

Then I heard another howl. Closer.

I wasn't sure which direction it was coming from. As I hurried along, I clutched my cell phone. My hands were shaking in the cold and in fear. I checked for a signal, but still nothing.

I heard a howl again. This time it seemed only yards away.

Being lost was one thing. If I could stay calm and possibly ride out the storm, I might be able to figure out the shortest route home. But this was deathly different. There wasn't time. I had to get out now—or not get out at all.

"Please help me!" I screamed again. "I'm lost!"

I only heard the sound of the wind and the tapping of the supersized flakes hitting the trees and ground and my own raspy breathing.

Then I heard a different howl. It couldn't be—another wolf? This time the howl seemed a few feet away and coming from another direction.

My heart accelerated. My teeth began to chatter, not because I was cold, but because I was scared to death. The silence only magnified my intense pangs of isolation. I'd never felt so alone and scared. I didn't want to die.

"Someone—please help me!" I screamed. "Help!"

I was blinded, lost, cold, and alone—only I wasn't as alone as I would have liked. Branches crunched and twigs crackled, and the sound of heavy breathing was near.

Then I heard a deep, maddening, and fiery growl. This time it was coming from behind me. I immediately stopped in my tracks, fear penetrating through me. Hesitantly, I turned.

Between the heavy-falling snow appeared a ghastly sight—four pairs of gray, beastly eyes.

I'd never been so close to wolves as I was now—not even in a zoo with a steel cage between us.

The wolves crept closer. I could see their wet noses and the breath coming from their snouts. They licked their lips.

Terror shot through me like piercing icicles. I quietly positioned my cell phone. Finally. A connection! My fingers shaking, I began to press the number nine. Then I managed to press the number one.

The leader of the pack growled, exposing his white fangs and black gums. Another wolf barked. Startled, I flinched. The phone fell into the snow.

I learned in Health and Safety class that in the unlikely event that a person encountered a wolf, the person should try to make themselves appear bigger. I stood on my tiptoes, which was difficult to do in the piling snow and my bulky, furry boots, and raised my hands in the air.

"Help!" I called. "Please, someone—help!"

I took a few steps backward, making sure I didn't turn my back on them. They paced back and forth, watching.

My arms became heavy; I couldn't keep them up much longer. I hummed a sweet tune to myself, hoping it would relax me and the wolves.

There was a break in the overcast sky. The full moon peeked out. Celestial and glowing, it radiated its magnificent brilliance as if it were trying to comfort me. But I was far from comforted.

The wolves weren't budging, and my circulation was draining out from my fingertips. It would only be moments until I'd have to bring down my arms, and then I knew they'd surely attack.

I felt a presence behind me and my breath stopped. Just like that, I was surrounded. I was frozen with fear, my heart pounding, my fingers still shaking, my lips quivering. I closed my eyes and began to pray. I wondered how my parents would find me—if they'd even find me. I imagined Ivy and Abby spending the next three years shopping without me and Nash finding comfort in someone else's arms. And I realized that in my seventeen years I hadn't experienced the one thing that had always eluded me—true love.

Then whatever that presence was jumped out from behind me. I covered my head and screamed.

I heard a lot of scuffling, growling, and howling. It took a few moments for me to even realize I wasn't in any physical pain. Was I already dead?

I peeked out from my defenses. I saw a figure holding a large tree branch.

The figure swung at the pack with the branch, running and chasing after the wolves. Growling and the horrible sounds of a struggle raged just beyond my sight. I prayed the man was okay, but I wasn't sure what was happening just a few yards away in the heavy snow. I heard a crunch, then a male voice yell. All at once, there was a smack and the sound of yelping. Then there was dead silence.

I didn't know if the person was alive. I didn't hear the wolves. I didn't hear the man.

I waited. I wondered if I should call out to him, but I was afraid this might excite the wolves if they were still there. I didn't know what to do next.

When I didn't hear a sound, I knew I had to do something. I decided to go farther into the woods and see what had happened. I was terrified of what I might find.

Just then, the figure emerged from behind a tree. The guy was alive, out of breath, and exhausted. The snow fell heavily, blocking me from seeing my rescuer. Then, all at once, striking blue eyes shone through the snow. I was even more shocked . . . it was Brandon Maddox.

I was so happy to see someone that I threw my hands up and cheered.

Brandon had been fighting the wolf pack with all his strength. The falling snow made it hard to see, the woods made it hard to navigate through, and the cold temperature made it hard to breathe.

I'd always thought Brandon was handsome, but now he looked even more magnificent.

"Are you . . . okay?" It was the first thing he asked.

"Am *I* okay? I wasn't the one fighting a pack of wolves."

Brandon tossed the branch into the woods. It was then a few dark red drops fell into the lily white snow.

"You're bleeding!" I said, pointing to the red stains.

"What?" He didn't even look at his hand. "What are you doing . . . here?" he asked. He was still running on adrenaline.

"You've been hurt," I said. "We should get you to a doctor."

He raised his hand. Drops continued to fall into the snow.

"You need to have that looked at," I said. "You might need stitches."

"It's nothing," he said.

"You could have rabies," I warned.

"I'm fine."

"Can I see?" I asked.

"Uh . . . sure."

I hadn't even spoken to Brandon before now, but words couldn't express the gratitude I felt discovering anyone—especially him—here with me in the woods. I'd always been drawn to Brandon, and his heroic actions only magnified my feelings. I slowly reached out to him. Our fingers touched and I melted.

I took his hand and held it in mine. It was strong and warm even though it was wet from the falling snow. I gently peeled back his ripped glove to examine the wound. There was a bloody gash in the palm of his hand.

"You've been bitten!" I said, alarmed. "You'll have to see a doctor. You don't want it to get infected."

"That's okay—" he said, trying to shrug off the seriousness of the wound.

"No, you must."

"I'm fine."

"But you're still bleeding. I'll bandage it for you." I dug my free hand into my purse and took out a pack of tissues. I applied a few tissues to his hand and unwound my scarf from around my neck. I could feel him staring at me as I tended to his wound. He examined my hair, my face, my lips. Gently, I wrapped the scarf around his hand and tucked in the ends.

We stood in the snow—in the middle of the woods, in the middle of Legend's Run. Brandon Maddox's hand in mine. Neither one of us was letting go.

"It's kind of bulky," I said, "but it will do for now."

I felt so tired. Now, knowing someone was with me, that I wasn't alone anymore and that I wasn't hurt, my body started to cave in. Brandon reached out and steadied me with his good hand.

"I could have been—" I said, realizing the severity of the situation. "But you—"

It was hard for me to get past the image that plagued my mind—if Brandon hadn't shown up when he did, I'd have been attacked by a pack of wolves. Instead, he had scared them off. But he'd been bitten.

"I'd take you to a doctor," I said. "But I don't even know where I am."

Then Brandon smiled—a terminally seductive smile. The kind smiled by A-list movie stars. The kind that takes one's breath away.

"I'll show you," he finally said.

I let go of his hand. As we started walking, the snowfall began to dwindle. I couldn't feel my hands, my feet, my legs. They all seemed numb from the event, somehow moving on their own.

The flakes became smaller and eventually were more sporadic as we walked in silence. He escorted me through the woods valiantly, as if he knew this piece of land as well as his own home.

We reached the snow-covered road. A few cars passed

by slowly, their tires splashing the wintry mix. I saw the roof of my house in the distance. I was closer to home than I'd thought.

"My house is just over there." I pointed to my subdivision. I was so happy to see my house, I had to fight back tears. "I don't know how to thank you. You . . . saved my life."

I turned around to embrace my hero, but Brandon had already disappeared.

EIGHT

rescued

I arrived home breathless, spaced out, and chilled to the bone.

"There you are!" my mom said, relieved. "Where have you been?"

I must have looked like a roughed-up snow angel. If I'd been skiing, sledding, or snowboarding—none of which my friends had time for anymore, and Ivy never liked anyway—I would have had layers of clothing, puffy gloves, earmuffs, a knit hat, and a down-filled coat.

But this time I was caught in the snow by accident and wasn't prepared for it.

"I've been worried sick," my mom said as I unzipped my now-white hoodie. Flakes fell on our tiled foyer. I shook the snow off my boots on an inside mat, but I couldn't feel a thing—my legs and toes were numb. Our dog, Champ, bounded up to me and sniffed my pant legs.

"I called several times," my mom continued, "but you didn't answer. I was just getting my keys to come and look for you."

I was so happy to be home, I was speechless. So much had just happened to me since I left Ivy and Abby, I couldn't process everything. All I knew was I was finally home.

My mom pulled off my gloves. "Your fingers are frozen." She warmed them in her hands.

"I got caught in that snowstorm."

"I can see that. Are Ivy and Abby okay?"

I nodded. "I think they missed the storm."

"They weren't with you?" she asked, surprised.

I leaned against the staircase railings and my mom pulled off my boots. I was too tired to hike the stairs to my room. Instead, I sat on them and peeled off my jeans. My mom handed me warm sweatpants and fuzzy slipper socks from the laundry room. Champ licked my cold fingers.

I'd never been so happy to be home in all my life. The smell of pasta wafting in from the kitchen was the most pleasant scent I could have imagined. It normally bothered me when my mom fussed over me, but I was so fatigued and cold, I welcomed her care.

I followed her into the family room. I plopped down on a sofa and she covered me with a fleece blanket, and Champ curled up at my feet.

My mom turned on our gas fireplace and I gladly gazed at our family pictures displayed on the mantel.

"Dinner's almost ready," she said.

I could hear her fiddling in the kitchen behind me, but I couldn't focus on what she was doing. I would have pinched myself to see if I was dreaming—being in the safety of my house with a fluffy family pet instead of staring at a pack of salivating wolves—only I still couldn't feel my skin.

"She just got home," I heard my mom tell my dad when he entered the house.

"That blizzard came out of nowhere," he said.

I was glad to see my dad and gave him puppy-dog eyes. He touched my face. Even though he'd been outside, his warm hand heated my chilled cheek.

"I think that caught us all off guard," he said.

"Dinner's ready," my mom called.

Still wrapped in my fleece blanket, I sat down at the dining table and immediately scarfed down an Italian roll.

"I didn't realize I'd been gone so long," I announced, glancing at the clock.

"Take your time," my mom said. "You don't want to choke."

"So why weren't you with Ivy?" my dad asked.

"I wanted to go straight home. But obviously that didn't happen."

"You walked home?" my dad asked.

"Yes. Then it started snowing and I ended up in the

woods. I saw a wolf. And just at the last moment—"

"What?" my dad asked. "Slow down. Why were you in the woods?"

"I got lost."

"Which woods?" my mom asked, just as concerned.

"The ones along Riverside."

"Riverside?" she asked, horrified. "What were you doing *there*? Where were Abby and Ivy?" my mom wondered.

"Ivy was driving Abby to her practice before tonight's game."

"This still doesn't make sense," my dad said. "What were you doing walking in Riverside alone?"

"Abby, Ivy, and I were getting our fortunes told."

"Didn't the psychic tell you you shouldn't go into the woods?" my dad asked, joking. "Seems obvious enough to me."

As a matter of fact, Dr. Meadows had warned me. *Beware of the woods . . . of the sounds of howling,* she had said. My stomach turned, and it wasn't from eating too fast. It was strange— her prediction. But it just had to be a coincidence, I assured myself.

"You didn't answer your cell phone," my mom said sharply. "I was about to drive around when you came in the door."

"I tried calling you—but I couldn't get a signal," I defended. "Then I dropped my phone in the snow. . . ." I realized I still didn't have my cell phone. "I'm really sorry— I think I lost it."

"Your cell phone can be replaced," she said.

"So . . . you said you saw a wolf?" my dad asked.

"Yes. Closer than I've ever seen."

"How close?" my mom asked.

"Only a few feet away. And it wasn't one wolf. It was a pack."

"You're so lucky they didn't see you," she said, relieved.

"See me? They almost ate me!"

My parents froze.

"They were as close to me as you both are and staring at me like you are now." As soon as I said that, I realized it was a mistake.

My mom covered her mouth. Then she took my hand. My dad's brows furrowed.

I could see by my parents' horrified expressions as they imagined their daughter being torn to shreds, I would be lucky if I was ever allowed out of the house again.

"Honey, I'm so happy you weren't bitten!" my mom said gratefully. "Or worse."

It was then I thought of Brandon. He *was* bitten and he didn't seem concerned. He'd been more interested in my well-being than his.

"It's odd to see a wolf up close like that—so close to town," my dad said. "They usually like to avoid people."

"I must have stumbled on their den. They didn't appear too happy to see me."

"I'd think their den would be farther outside of town. That's where they're mostly spotted," my dad added.

"I don't know," I said, taking a drink. "I only know I saw them and they saw me."

"Are you sure they were wolves?" my mom pressed.

"Do squirrels have fangs?" I asked.

"Well, we're glad you're back home safe," my mom continued.

"I'm not a forest ranger," I said. "I just know what I saw. I've never seen wolves up close. It was terrifying!"

That hit my mom hard. She always wanted to protect me, and I knew it hurt her to have me be in a situation where I'd been afraid and alone.

"I'm so sorry I wasn't there—" she said.

"How did you manage to make it out?" my dad asked. "Alive? Without a scratch?"

My parents waited for my answer.

A guy saved me. Risked his life for mine. A handsome Westsider.

I was too exhausted to tell them any more, and it would only add to their endless questions. I always told my parents the truth, no matter what the truth was, but in this case I felt funny about telling them about Brandon. I knew they'd make a fuss—show up at his house, thank him, and insist on taking him out to dinner. It would be embarrassing for him, and I wanted to spare him the gushing parental gratitude. So instead I just skipped to the end. "The snow began to let up. Eventually I could see our house."

"Well, thank goodness it did!" My mom sighed. "Thank goodness it did."

"I still don't understand why you were getting your fortunes told," my dad said. "Don't you girls have homework to do?"

"It was sort of a dare," I tried to explain.

"What did the psychic say?" my mom asked.

"It's private," I said. "Like making a wish on your birthday."

"Did she say we were going to win the lottery?" my mom asked. "Or travel the world?"

"No. She didn't say anything about becoming rich or winning a fabulous vacation," I replied.

"Well, I'm so happy you are safe," my mom said.

"I second that," my father affirmed. "And here's a fortune for you," he said, directing his attention toward me. "No walking by yourself outside our subdivision anymore. Or you'll be grounded."

High school basketball games were one of the biggest events in the Legend's Run social calendar. There wasn't much else to do in town, and our team usually put on quite a performance. Almost everyone in town attended the games—except for one person.

When I arrived at the game, I scanned the bleachers for Brandon. I saw a few Westsiders, but no heroes.

Ivy was waiting for me by the snack stand. The smell of hot dogs, hot chocolate, and popcorn was almost intoxicating.

I was bursting to tell her my harrowing story. "You'll never believe what happened on my way home," I said.

"Were you mugged? I knew I shouldn't have left you!"

"No—I got lost."

"Lost? You were just down the road from your house."

"There was a snowstorm on the Westside and I got caught in it."

"Really? We must have just missed it."

"Well, I didn't, and I got disoriented and found myself in the middle of the woods."

"What woods?"

"The ones that run along Riverside."

Ivy was horrified. "You could have been killed—you don't know who lives in there."

"No one was *living* in there," I assured her.

"So what happened?"

"There was a pack of wolves—so close I could see their wet noses!"

Ivy paused. I wasn't sure she believed me. This wasn't the usual "girl meets friend, friends go to mall" story.

"Really?" she asked skeptically.

"Yes! Why don't people believe me?"

"What people?"

"My family. Now you."

"We all believe you," she affirmed.

"I've never lied before."

"I know that," she said. "It's just that if you met a pack of wolves in the woods, how are you standing here telling me about it?"

She had a point. There was that one significant detail I was leaving out. The detail with the royal blue eyes.

"So, how did you escape the wolves?" she asked.

"Well . . ."

"Yes?"

"Uh . . . They eventually heard some noises and ran off." It was mostly true.

"Thank goodness!" She gave me a quick hug. "Now, that's the last time we'll be going to Riverside!"

I didn't have to share every detail of my day with my family and best friend. Perhaps there are some things worth keeping close to one's own heart.

Nash, Jake, and Dylan were doing their pregame warm-ups on the court. Abby was chatting with a few cheerleaders stretching out in the corner and waved us over.

The guys were handsome in their blue-and-gold jerseys and shorts. Nash began discussing plays with the coach while Jake and Dylan continued warming up. While Ivy told Abby my story, I scanned the crowd for Brandon.

"You were lost in the woods?" Abby asked, breaking me out of my trance. "Can I call you Red? Just like your costume on Halloween. You are *so* her."

"What?" I asked.

"Little Red Riding Hood. But instead of one wolf, you encountered many."

"Seems as if I did," I said.

"Then how did you get out?" she asked. "They could have killed you!"

"I know."

"Celeste says they just retreated," Ivy answered for me.

"Just like that?" Abby asked.

"I don't really want to talk about it."

"Didn't Dr. Meadows say something freaky about you and the woods and a wolf?" Abby remembered.

"She did!" Ivy said.

"That didn't mean anything," I insisted.

"She warned you!" Abby said with a voodoo glare. "She *is* psychic."

As the buzzer sounded, the three of us climbed the bleachers and watched our beaux take on the Highland Valley Bears.

I wasn't a big fan of basketball, but I did like the sport's fast pace, and Legend's Run High had a great team. Although my mind would occasionally drift from one free throw to another, I used some of that time to jot down ideas and thoughts in my spiral binder. But tonight, I had only three things on my mind—the woods, the wolves, and Brandon. I wasn't even sure throughout the game which team was winning. All I could see was Brandon's blue eyes shining through the snow when I thought I was on death's doorstep;

his fearless heroics and selfless humility; his coming to my aid like a brave knight does for a princess in peril.

The game finally came to an end, and the Legend's Run Wolverines were victorious over the Bears. I couldn't help but be disillusioned. Nash's final swish got more fanfare than a guy in the woods who saved a girl's life.

I watched Nash, Dylan, and Jake tear into chicken and sodas at Wings and Things while my friends and I listened to them retelling their final play of the game. But I didn't have an appetite. I had butterflies in the pit of my stomach. I felt as if I'd never be able to eat again.

"What's up?" Nash finally said to me.

Abby told him my story. By this time it was thirdhand. Even with her embellishments, the end was still the same— I'd been as close to a pack of wolves' dinner as these chicken wings were to our boyfriends' mouths.

"And that psychic predicted the whole thing?"

"Even what she was wearing," Abby said.

"She did not—" I tried to tell them.

"What else did she say?" Jake prodded.

The gang waited for my answer. I wasn't about to tell them the rest.

"I don't remember," I said.

"Something about an outsider," Ivy chimed in.

"Yes, an outsider," Abby repeated.

"Did you see an outsider there?" Jake asked. "I wonder what that means."

I wasn't about to tell them that I did see an outsider—that he was from the Westside and had the best eyes I'd ever seen.

"Your girlfriend was only moments from the clutches of death!" Jake teased Nash.

"It's true," Ivy defended. "She was surrounded by a pack of wolves."

"Wolves?" The color washed out of Nash's face.

"Yes, wolves," Abby said, stressing the severity of the situation.

"The Big Bad Wolf?" Nash teased, recovering his cool. "So how did you get out?"

I could tell my friends right there and then that the wolves didn't retreat but rather were fought off by someone who didn't run away from wolves or wasn't frightened by the mere mention of their species. But as the words came to my mouth, I saw that the story might hurt Nash. Once word spread throughout school that there was a real hero in Legend's Run, the star of the football and basketball teams could never measure up to that feat. And once it was discovered that someone, especially an unpopular Westsider, saved Nash's girlfriend's life—something he didn't do and possibly could never do—it could ruin Nash's reputation and ego for the rest of our days at Legend's Run High.

"So . . . how did you survive it?" Nash pressed.

"I raised my hands like they told me in school and the wolves eventually went away."

"What woods were you in?" he asked.

"The ones in Riverside," Abby answered.

"Why were you in Riverside?" Nash asked.

Abby waved her receipt in his face. "Servants for a day! Starting tomorrow! Not only am I going to get an A on my English project, but I'm going to get a free massage, too."

Dylan rolled his eyes.

"And what do I have to do?" Jake asked.

"I'll let you know when we're alone," Ivy said.

"Don't get too excited," Dylan whispered. "For some reason, I think it has to do with shopping."

"And me?" Nash asked. "I'm not going into the woods again. Especially with you. You seem to attract wolves."

"We'll be indoors," I said. "This time, you'll have to invite someone who *isn't* on one of your teams."

Maybe this was a small gesture for an outsider—to be finally included in the popular students' party.

Nash drove me home. When I unbuckled my seat belt, he leaned over. For some reason, I turned away. His lips landed softly on my cheek.

"What's wrong?" he asked.

"Nothing." I hopped out of the car before he could question me anymore. As usual, Nash didn't walk me to the front door but sped off when I unlocked it and stepped inside.

Wolves weren't the only thing on my mind as I tried desperately to fall asleep. I felt attracted to Brandon Maddox like I hadn't been drawn to anyone ever before—not Nash, or even a movie or TV star I'd adored. I replayed the late afternoon's harrowing event in my mind—that at the last second before I was about to be wolf bait, a handsome hero swooped into the most dangerous situation of my life and saved me from the clutches of death. I wasn't sure why I felt so strongly for Brandon—someone who I didn't really know much about— but I did. Perhaps it was the same feeling a victim has toward a firefighter or police officer who saves them in the line of duty.

I recalled the moment when Brandon and I stood together underneath the romantic snowfall and in the solitude of the woods, our bodies close together and our hands entwined. I didn't want to let go. Not then. Not ever.

I was excited. I could barely breathe. I had butterflies fluttering through my body. My heart ached. I wanted to dance around my room for days.

I thought about him staring at me when I bandaged his hand and holding me when I felt dizzy. I imagined my scarf, wrapped around his hand; how lucky it was to be so close to him.

The more I tried to get Brandon out of my mind, the more he infiltrated it. My soft blue fleece blanket reminded me of his eyes. The winter scarves hanging in my closet only further reminded me of the one I'd secured on his bitten hand. The full moon shining through my bedroom window was the same one that had hovered over us as he fought off the threatening wolves.

It didn't hurt that Brandon was handsome, enigmatic, and strong. I rationalized that I was just swept up in the moment. Maybe in time this emotional connection would dissipate like the snowfall. The clouds would break and I'd be free of this feeling, just as I was finally free from the woods themselves.

I wasn't sure why I was thinking of Brandon when I was currently dating Nash. I was lucky enough to be going out with the star of the basketball team and best friend to my friends' boyfriends. My parents loved him, and so did everyone at school.

Besides, why would Brandon have feelings for me? I was just some girl he heard crying in the woods and decided to help her. I could have been anyone. But when we held hands and he smiled at me, I felt a connection that I'd never experienced before.

And at the end of his heroics, he was left wounded and bloody. I couldn't help but be concerned. His once-healthy hand was mauled and I was the cause. If I hadn't been so insistent on walking home alone, I wouldn't have gotten lost and he wouldn't have been bitten.

I tossed and turned and gazed into the moonlight streaming through my curtain and into the darkness of my room. Eventually these crazy love-struck thoughts that possessed me would surely go away and I'd return to daydreaming and writing in my notebook about the moon and the stars.

I recalled Nash's reaction to hearing the cry of a wolf only a few months ago. The two events in the woods mirrored each other. When Nash had told the story of the werewolf, he ran off, frightened by his own tale. Brandon, on the other hand, had risked his life for mine and jumped into a real life-and-death situation without hesitation. Not only didn't Nash think of me when he was hightailing it back to his car, but he wasn't thinking of his other friends, either.

Did that make Nash a bad person? Maybe I wasn't being fair to him. No one in their right mind wanted to confront a pack of wolves. I wondered what made someone have the instinct of flight while others had the courage to fight.

I'd never be able to admit my doughy, in-love-with-a-Westsider feeling to Ivy or Abby. Brandon didn't fit neatly into their clique. To them, he was an outsider, plain and simple. He didn't live in our neighborhood, he didn't play sports, and, most important, he wasn't Nash.

For now, I'd have to keep my thoughts and feelings locked away inside me. If Brandon didn't tell anyone about the event, and neither did I, then no one would be the wiser.

However, I knew I'd need to thank Brandon. If Nash had rescued someone, he'd want to make it known and be celebrated on national TV. Brandon, however, had disappeared. I didn't even know where he lived to deliver him a thank-you gift. I assumed he didn't want any recognition or attention. I felt he might be the kind of person who'd be embarrassed if I tried. Besides, what does one do for a person who saves one's life? Brandon was a true hero—brave, modest, humble.

There was no real way to properly thank them. But that didn't mean I shouldn't try.

For now, I'd just have to wait for the right moment.

I wouldn't be able to admit my obsessive feelings toward Brandon to anyone—not my friends, family, or him—when it was hard enough to admit them to myself. Instead I looked at the clock and counted the minutes until I knew I'd see him again.

NINE

tall tales

I wasn't excited about the weekend. Normally, I'd take advantage of the two days off catching up on homework, chores, and, most of all, texting, calling, and hanging out with Ivy and Abby. Nash had an away game, so we weren't going to have a date night. I was so eager to go back to school and see Brandon, I spent most of my hours not accomplishing anything and dreaming about him.

I tried to snap myself out of my pining for Brandon, so I threw myself into the research for my folklore paper. Werewolves were subjects of Greek mythology and European and Early American folklore. In most of the traditions, lycanthropes were scary, deadly creatures to be feared. No one wanted to become a werewolf, and no one wanted to encounter one. I'd been holed up all day when I thought it might be good to get some new perspective. Mr. Worthington seemed to know more than anyone about the legends, and I knew he'd be happy to tell me about them.

"I want to talk about werewolves," I said when I found him reading a magazine in the lobby at Pine Tree Village later that day. "I'm doing a paper on folklore and thought you'd be the perfect person to interview."

He paused, taking an extra moment to examine me. Then he closed his magazine.

"It's me, Celeste," I said, confused at his expression.

"I know who you are . . ." he said cheekily. "But you seem different. . . ."

"What do you mean?"

"There's an extra twinkle in your eye."

I blushed. Could he see I'd been obsessed about Brandon?

"I'm not sure what you mean," I said.

"Are you sure there isn't anything new? Did you do something different to your hair?"

"Same old me," I said. I felt funny about girl talking and gushing about a guy I couldn't get out of my mind to an eighty-nine-year-old man.

"I'll get it out of you eventually," he said. "Something about you . . . but I can't put my finger on it. I haven't been around for all these years without seeing things."

"Well, that is what I want to talk to you about."

"Yes?"

"I'm doing a paper on werewolf folklore and was hoping you could tell me more about the Legend's Run werewolf."

Mr. Worthington perked up.

"Please, come sit down."

I sat on the sofa next to him. I pulled out my notebook and opened it on my lap. "I read that a person could become a werewolf if they wear a pelt or skin from a wolf," I said, "or if they're bitten by a werewolf. And of course one of the cures is a silver bullet."

"Go on," he said.

"And some can shape-shift."

"Yes."

"But that's all basic stuff. I want to know—what do you know about the Legend's Run werewolf?"

"What do I know?" he said with a mischievous laugh.

"Yes. Anything you can tell me would be great."

"Well, let's see," Mr. Worthington began. "He was first spotted in the last century, soon after the town was founded. But his transformation didn't come from a werewolf bite or a pelt of skin worn around his human body. It came from the bite of a wolf."

"Wow . . ." I said.

"He was a regular man—in fact, a good man—one of the early settlers who were helping build the community. A loved and respected man." Mr. Worthington recited his tale as if it were fact. "He was building a house when a pack of rabid wolves stole the basket his child was resting in. The man fought for his son's life. In the struggle, the man was left bloody and fighting for his life. The following full moon, the man was missing from his home. It was very unusual, as he was always protective of his family and community."

"Did they find him?"

"No one knew where he was. But then bad things began to happen in the town. Animals suddenly went missing and people feared the dark. A frightening creature, half man, half wolf, was spotted prowling in the woods, and townspeople heard howling throughout the night."

I hung on to his every word. "Creepy."

"But the terror didn't happen just once a month. The moon can appear full for several evenings. And during that time, no one is safe when there is a werewolf among us."

"Wow—you know more than Nash did. This is great."

"I was just at the beginning."

"The beginning? What happened to the man?"

Nurse Bridget interrupted our conversation.

"Hi, Celeste, I didn't know you were scheduled today."

"Uh . . . I wasn't. I just came over to interview Mr. Worthington for a paper I'm working on for school."

"Well, I'm afraid it's time for Charlie's physical therapy. I hope it isn't something due tomorrow."

"It's not due till the next full moon," I said to Mr. Worthington with a wink.

* * *

I'd been so enthralled with Mr. Worthington's story, I didn't even write anything down in my notebook. I transcribed all my memories into my computer when I arrived home. If Mr. Worthington was only at the beginning of his story, what more did he know?

As I finished editing my interview, I remembered Dr. Meadows's prediction. If we hadn't gone to Penny for Your Thoughts in the first place, then I wouldn't have gotten lost in the woods and Brandon wouldn't have been bitten. Was her reading correct? The idea that Dr. Meadows predicted exactly what happened plagued my mind. But then again, I convinced myself that any person could have said those things, psychic or not. Maybe she had heard the weather forecast. Maybe she knew that wolves were inhabiting the Westside woods. Or any client could interpret events to match their psychic's words.

But, if in fact she had truthfully warned me, was I the one to blame for Brandon's injury? If only I'd not been so skeptical and listened to her, he wouldn't have put himself in harm's way and have gotten hurt.

Either way, I felt guilty for putting him in a position that led to his getting wounded.

And what did Dr. Meadows mean by *Beware of a kiss under the full moon. It can change your life forever.* Perhaps she was talking about the paper I was currently writing? Maybe writing this paper would change me. And did she mean kisses I might receive from Nash or wanted to receive from Brandon? For some reason, or many (getting to know more about Mr. Worthington and investigating the paranormal), I felt it already had.

I shut down my computer. I was so excited the weekend was over and school was going to be in session tomorrow. As I lay in bed, I jotted the memories down in my notebook as I replayed them in my head: Brandon suddenly appearing out of the snow, like a firefighter coming out of the flames, his royal blue eyes melting me and the snow and ice around us, our hands touching as if we'd never let go.

I closed my notebook and held it to my heart as I fell asleep.

athletes and apologies

When I arrived in English class I spotted a shiny object lying on my desk. As I drew closer, I realized it was my cell phone.

"Someone found it!" Ivy said, discovering it, too.

Brandon wasn't in class, but his backpack was leaning against his desk.

Just then Brandon sauntered into class. He was wearing an NHL jersey over an oatmeal-colored thermal and black fingerless gloves. I thought it was quite a cool look, but I knew the gloves were to cover up the horrible mauling he'd received a few days before. I felt such sympathy for him and the wound he'd incurred, but I also felt electrified by his presence. An immediate buzzing tingled all over my skin. Before I knew it, I was oversmiling and hypertalking to Ivy as if I were onstage performing for an audience. I didn't even know why I was doing it, but I couldn't help myself.

I didn't dare make contact—eye, verbal, or any other kind. Brandon must have felt the same. In my peripheral vision, I saw him take his seat. I was dying to see if he noticed me.

Instead, I held the cell phone in my hand. I imagined where it had been. In his coat pocket? Maybe at his home by his bed. At some point, he had held it in his hand, as I was doing now.

I was such a love-struck girl and yet I couldn't control my ridiculous feelings.

Finally, I put the phone in my back pocket.

"Not so fast," Mrs. Clark said. It was against school rules to have a cell phone in class. And though I was a good student, Mrs. Clark wasn't about to bend the rules for me. "I'll return it to you after class."

Abby whispered to Ivy. Then Ivy whispered to me. "Brandon is wearing fingerless gloves."

"So?" I said.

"Don't you think it's odd?"

"No. It is cold out," I defended.

"Maybe he got a tat," Abby said.

"On his hand?" I asked.

"On his knuckles," Abby corrected.

"Yes, that's big with the juvies," Ivy said.

"There is no evidence he's a juvie," I said. "You both watch too much TV."

"He's just not like us," Abby said. "It's like he doesn't want to fit in with the rest of us—or even try to."

"Why should he?" I asked. "It's not like anyone is overly friendly toward him."

"I think he's trying to hide something," Ivy theorized. "He doesn't make eye contact, he sits alone, and now he's all about coats and gloves in class."

"Yes . . . I'm sure that's it," I said. "Has to be hiding something, otherwise it's not worth discussing."

"You are so right," Ivy said with a smile.

"What could it be?" Abby asked.

I was the only one who knew what Brandon was hiding. And I wasn't about to tell.

By lunchtime, Jake and Dylan were showing signs of strain, trailing Ivy and Abby and holding their girlfriends' trays, backpacks, and purses. The students laughed as they passed by, and so did I. They were doing their best to live up to "servants for a day."

Nash grabbed a burger from the line and passed Brandon.

"Hey, dude—what's with the gloves?" Nash said. "We are inside, you know."

Brandon paused. I wasn't sure what he was going to say. *I'm hiding a wound I received while saving your girlfriend's life? Didn't she already tell you?*

But he didn't answer.

"Wolf got your tongue?" Nash challenged.

"Don't be rude!" I said to Nash.

"I was just wondering, is that the new fashion in Riverside?" Nash asked.

Abby, Ivy, Dylan, and Jake remained at Nash's side. Brandon was alone.

"You can tell me," Nash said.

Brandon remained silent.

"Or maybe you're trying to hide something," Nash taunted.

I pulled Nash away.

"Sorry. He got an A in football but an F in manners," I said to Brandon. I continued to lead Nash back to our usual table.

We sat down and Jake and Dylan began cutting my friends' salads.

"You aren't going to feed them, too, are you?" Nash asked.

"I hadn't thought of that," Abby said with a laugh.

"So what did you have Nash do as your servant?" Ivy asked.

"So far, nothing." He grinned triumphantly. "And the day is half over."

"Nothing?" Dylan asked, outraged.

I'd thought about it all day. What would I make Nash do? I could carry my own purse and backpack. I guess the point was to humiliate them and be able to order them around like we couldn't normally. Nash wasn't used to taking orders, and I wasn't used to giving them. I was the kind that let my opponent win a board game for fear they might feel bad if they lost.

"You have to make him do something," Jake urged.

"Yes, and it better be good," Dylan threatened.

"Okay. Okay," I finally said.

My friends waited for my command. Nash tensed up, sure I was going to order him to run naked through the cafeteria. I wasn't sure, however, if he'd object to such a stunt.

"I told you I want you to have a party," I said.

"That's it?" Nash replied happily. "I always have parties. No big deal."

"That's not all," I said. "I haven't provided you with the guest list."

"Oh. Is it boys only?" Jake asked. "You getting to hang out with the entire basketball team?"

"No, maybe it's only Nash," Dylan said.

"That's not much of a party," Jake said.

"Yeah?" Nash finally said.

"You'll invite the usual crowd. Plus one special guest."

"Who's that?" he asked.

"You were just talking to him," I said. "Brandon. The guy with fingerless gloves."

"Are you kidding?" Nash asked, slapping the table.

"That's not it," I said. "I want you to march over there and apologize to him for your behavior. And then, invite him to your party."

"You want me to kiss him, too?"

"Now, that's a good idea!" Dylan said.

I was beaming. Even my best friends were thrilled.

"Wow—we had it easy," Jake said. "You have to apologize to a Westsider in front of the whole school."

"Apologize for what?" Nash was fuming.

"Hey, man, we lived up to our bargain," Dylan said. "Now it's your turn."

"I don't want that jerk running around my house," Nash said. "What if he steals something?"

"What if he doesn't?" I replied.

"You're kidding me, right?" he said.

I shook my head. My friends grinned.

We watched as Nash rose and headed over to Brandon. As Nash got close to Brandon's table, the other students, one by one, became aware of the unusual occurrence and watched with awe.

When Nash reached Brandon's table, Brandon appeared skeptical.

The whole lunchroom was prepared for a fight.

"Hey, dude—" Nash began. "I'm . . . uh . . ." He cleared his throat. "About the glove comment . . ."

Brandon rose.

Nash looked back at me. I nodded.

Then he turned to Brandon. "I'm sorry."

Brandon was as surprised as the rest of the lunchroom. The staff even breathed sighs of relief, knowing that they wouldn't have to break up a fight.

"No problem," Brandon finally said.

"And I'm having a party this weekend," Nash continued painfully. "You can bring some friends."

"Uh . . . Okay—"

Nash pulled a face as he walked over to us.

Brandon gazed at me, and I couldn't help but smile in return.

I sat at my computer and attempted to work on my essay on folklore and distract myself from my Brandon Maddox obsession. The bite of a wolf. The full moon. A howl on a dark and dreary night. Everything wolf-related only reminded me of him more.

As if that wasn't enough, I'd been clinging to my cell phone, the very same one he possessed. I'd never felt this guy-crazy before.

"Why don't you put that down?" my mom said that evening at dinner. I had my fork in one hand and my phone in the other.

"I'm afraid I may lose it," I said.

"I think you might be a little overprotective of it. I'm glad you found it, but it's not necessary to hold it twenty-four/seven," my mom said.

I tried my best to eat, but my stomach was in knots. Ever since we'd gone to Penny for Your Thoughts, I felt like my life was out of control. First the wolves in the snowstorm,

Brandon Maddox rescuing me, his wound, and now my ridiculous obsession with him. I couldn't help but blame Dr. Meadows and her strange fortune for getting me into this situation in the first place. What exactly had she said? *Beware of the woods . . . of the sounds of howling. There could be outsiders who will turn . . . underneath the glow of the full moon.* And then, when she'd grabbed me on the way out the door, she'd added, *Beware of a kiss under the full moon. It will change your life forever.*

The snow. The woods. Howling. A full moon. Could she have really seen the strange events before they unfolded? Maybe not. It was November, so it wasn't that unforeseen that it might snow. Legend's Run had a wolf population, so seeing one wouldn't be as shocking as coming upon a zebra. And the moon? It was full twelve times a year. But a kiss? Brandon Maddox was the outsider, but I could only dream of kissing him. What did that part of the prediction mean?

I imagined the party Nash was going to host. This time, since he'd lost the dare, he'd have to be as kind to his Riverside guests as he was to his own players on the field. This could be a big step for Nash, opening his home to someone outside his comfort zone. Nash usually only thought about himself. Maybe this would be an opportunity for him to expand his tightly knit social circle. An opportunity for him to grow. If Nash could get along with Brandon, maybe at last the Westside and Eastside could be Oneside.

dare to party

A few days later, the fire alarm rang during U.S. History class. I loved a good fire drill—it disrupted class for the time being, gave us a chance for some fresh air, and allowed Ivy, Abby, and me the freedom to gossip.

The only problem was when the high school performed the drills in a season with plummeting temperatures. It was always on a day when I chose not to drag my coat with me all day and kept it in my locker. The guys didn't seem bothered by not wearing their coats, but I was freezing. Our class lined up outside where the asphalt met the grass. Nash, Dylan, and Jake used the opportunity to throw snowballs.

"Here, you're shivering." Brandon was holding out his coat to me.

I was taken aback at his kind gesture. Nash hadn't

even offered to stand next to me. I think I was too cold to answer.

I wanted so badly to be wrapped in Brandon's coat, but I knew if I took it, my friends would freak out—especially Nash. But what my friends and Nash didn't know was that I wanted to use Brandon's coat—not because I was cold, but because it was *his* coat. It was close to his skin and cloaked him all day long. I knew it would smell good, too—like fabric softener or irresistible cologne or smoke from a fireplace. I wanted to wear it now, wear it all day, wear it forever. It would be the closest I'd be able to get to him again, since our time together in the woods when he saved my life.

Ivy shot me a dirty look. She was protective of me and must have thought Brandon was hitting on me. I could only hope.

Abby yanked my sleeve toward her and the three of us girls huddled together.

"I'll take it," Hayley Phillips, a skater from Riverside, said. She was wearing fingerless gloves, a knit hat, and a long-sleeved thermal henley. She put on Brandon's coat. It swallowed her up like an oversized blanket.

I envied her. At that moment I would have given anything to have been in her skateboarding shoes.

School was closed for the next few days for the Thanksgiving holiday. Since I couldn't see Brandon at school, I was looking forward to Nash's party in the hope that he might show up. Nash lived in the same subdivision as Ivy and Abby. The homes were estates and had as many bathrooms as bedrooms. I spent hours trying to find the perfect outfit. I realized I was dressing up as much for a possible Brandon sighting as I was for Nash.

There was a strong chance Brandon wouldn't show. Not only might it be that he'd gone out of town for the holiday, but if he'd remained in Legend's Run, what did he have to gain by attending? He didn't socialize with any of us or anyone who was coming to the party. He might have thought it was a trick or a potential hazing.

Ivy and I arrived at the party to find Abby already there with Dylan. Jake was talking to several jocks, and Nash was nowhere to be found.

When we headed into the kitchen, I found Nash by the refrigerator. Instead of greeting me with a passionate kiss— which I would have been uncomfortable with anyway—he seemed almost put off by my presence.

"You want me to pour your drinks?" He sighed. "I'm not used to being someone's servant, you know. I thought I did my job when I apologized to that guy. Anyway, I haven't seen him, and I'm crossing my fingers he doesn't show."

"Well, I think pouring me a soda would be a nice gesture," I said, not because I wanted him to be a servant, but because it was the gentlemanly thing to do. "But I can pour my own drink," I finally said.

"Forget it—" Nash said. "I'm not being a good host.

What would you ladies like?"

I knew there was a good guy inside of Nash, but sometimes it took a lot of prodding to find him.

I hoped Brandon would arrive at any moment. There was a chance we could all get to know one another and make him feel more comfortable at our school. I knew that our being one big happy clique was near to impossible, but it was my nature to dream.

An hour passed and Brandon still hadn't shown.

"You seem distracted," Ivy said. "This party was your idea. You should be having the most fun."

"I got the best part of the dare," Nash said, chuckling. "Shame that Westsider didn't show. I'm sure we would have been great friends."

Nash headed for the stairs. I didn't even follow him. Instead I sat on the couch and vacantly watched whatever was playing on the TV. The clock ticked on and Nash didn't return. I'd finished my soda hours ago, so I decided to get a bottle of water. I was headed back to the kitchen when I spotted Brandon in the corner of the parlor.

He looked magnetic—more stunning than any other guy there. It wasn't hard for him to look gorgeous—for Brandon it came naturally. It was clear he could have any girl at the party, if one so much as saw beyond his Westsider status. But it didn't seem likely that any of these girls would look past their turned-up noses, and for this, I was almost grateful. He would have been fawned all over by every cheerleader and become just like any other guy on the football or basketball team, possibly just like the one who had invited me—who was supposed to be my boyfriend and wasn't paying me any attention.

Brandon was sitting with Hayley Phillips and a few other skaters whom he must have brought with him. Hayley was talking to her friends, but Brandon wasn't listening to their conversation. I didn't think they were dating—I hoped they weren't. Brandon wasn't really talking to them but rather he appeared like he was observing the crowd, as if he was looking for someone. He didn't notice me watching him.

"We should talk to them," I said when Ivy reached my side.

"Why?" Ivy asked.

"Because they were invited to the party."

"I know it's your nature to be nice to everyone. But really, we don't know them. They seem to be really happy hanging out together. And besides, it's Nash's party, not ours. He's the one who should talk to them."

Then it hit me—what if Brandon did mention our time in the woods? My friends would be very curious why I hadn't mentioned that he was the one who saved me. Maybe I didn't want my friends talking to them—I wasn't sure they would understand why I hadn't told them myself, and I didn't want there to be trouble between Brandon and Nash.

On the other hand, Nash needed to welcome his new guests, just as Ivy said. I scoured the house for him. I went upstairs to find his bedroom door closed. Afraid of what—or who—I might find with him on the other side, I knocked. When no one answered, I opened it. The room was empty. I was relieved.

I finally found Nash downstairs in the media room. He was hanging out on the couch, yucking it up for some of his teammates. Heidi Rosen's legs were draped over his lap.

Brandon wasn't the only one Nash wasn't paying attention to.

Nash saw me standing at the bottom of the stairs. "Hey, Celeste—" he called.

I turned around and left. When I reached the top of the stairs, I bumped into Brandon. I didn't know what to say. I wanted to leave. My so-called boyfriend had disappointed me. I didn't want anyone, much less Brandon, to witness it.

I just wanted to go. I found Ivy and told her what I'd seen. "The thing is, Ivy. I'm not sure that I care," I finally admitted.

"Then you should stay," she encouraged.

"I mean about Nash."

Nash found me as I headed to the front door with my purse and keys in hand.

He tried to stop me.

"Celeste—" Nash said, "where are you going?"

"Out for some fresh air," I said.

"You misinterpreted what you saw," he said. "She was hanging on me, not the other way around."

"Whatever. I don't care. And besides, that's not the issue, Nash. You missed the whole point of this party," I said to him. "It was about our friends. It was about meeting other people. It definitely wasn't supposed to be about Heidi Rosen."

Fortunately the partygoers were focused on their own conversations—except for one person. Brandon was hanging by the foyer and overheard everything.

"Celeste, don't go," Ivy said, running up to us at the door. I pushed past Nash.

I was briskly marching to my car when I sensed someone behind me.

"I'm not staying, Nash," I said.

It wasn't Nash trailing me. It was Brandon.

He stood by my car, the moonlight shining on his face. He was so alluring, my heart raced and I was breathless. It was one thing to see Brandon from across the classroom or hallway, before he saved my life. But since I'd spent so many hours obsessing about him and imagining him kissing me, I was suddenly embarrassed being in his company—as if he knew the romantic thoughts I'd been thinking.

"Leaving so soon?" he asked.

"Uh . . . yes. I just . . ."

Now I felt torn. I was the one who put Nash up to inviting Brandon. Nash was ignoring him and now I was leaving.

"Funny. You were the reason I came," he said as if the words had slipped from his lips.

I didn't know what to say. I felt so flattered, awkward, and nervous. I knew I should say something witty back, but all my words escaped me.

I saw Nash looming by the front door.

"I better go," I said. As I got into my car, Nash went back inside.

Brandon watched me as I put the gear into reverse.

I wasn't sure what to do. I was pulled in two directions. I might have been leaving Nash, but I didn't want to leave Brandon.

I turned off the ignition and got out of the car.

"Did you forget something?" Brandon asked.

"I never properly thanked you," I said.

The moon twinkled above and the stars shined brightly. If I were the star of a Hollywood movie, I would have thrown myself into his arms and we would have shared a steamy kiss. But my life was far from a movie. I didn't move, and neither did Brandon.

"Celeste!" Ivy called. She and Abby were running toward me.

Brandon retreated into the darkened shadows of the front yard.

"I thought you already left," Ivy said. "I'm so glad you changed your mind."

"I just forgot something," I said.

"What did you forget?" Abby wondered.

"To thank someone who saved my life."

"I'm not sure what you mean," she said.

"That's okay." I sighed. "It's hard to explain."

"Please don't leave," Ivy begged. "Nash was just being foolish. He's in there sulking. You left him in front of everyone."

I smiled. Normally I didn't seek revenge, but Nash deserved a time-out. He wasn't doting like Jake and Dylan, or chivalrous like Brandon. I didn't want to be anywhere near him and remind myself of his behavior.

"Next time I have servants for a day," I said to Ivy, "I won't waste it on him."

TWELVE

skating partner

That night all I thought about was Brandon. I wondered what would have happened if Ivy hadn't interrupted us. Would I have gotten to talk to him more? I didn't know anything about him. Why did he move to Legend's Run? Did he really live with his grandparents? And most important, now that I was apart from Nash, would he ever kiss me?

I imagined what that moment would have been like gazing up at him as the stars glimmered behind him. I'd ask about his wound and he'd assure me it was nothing, all the while knowing that he was hiding his pain from me. And while no one was watching, he'd lean into me and kiss me so intensely I'd feel dizzy.

* * *

It was time to officially thank Brandon. I'd been putting it off perhaps for the wrong reasons—Nash, school, or just being shy. Brandon hadn't hesitated to save me, and I needed to move beyond any more hesitating in thanking him.

I didn't know much about Brandon, but I knew he liked Jeeps and the WWF.

The next day, I scanned the internet for images of pro wrestlers. When I found one I thought was beefy enough, I printed it out and glued it to card stock. I folded the card and wrote inside, *Thanks for wrestling the wolves. You are a true hero.*

I struggled with how to sign it. Sincerely? Best? Love? XOXO?

Just to be safe, I simply wrote *Celeste*. Before I put it in the envelope, I sprayed it with sweet perfume and stuck it into my purse.

I ran downstairs to check on the brownies I had baking in the oven. I took the hot dessert out and was sprinkling powdered sugar over it when Juliette and my mom entered the kitchen. It was cool to have my sister home for a few days, even if was just because my mom glowed having her two girls under her roof again.

"Why are you baking more desserts when we have pecan and pumpkin pies coming out of our ears?" Juliette said.

"Those smell delicious," my mom said.

"Why are you doing that to me?" Juliette complained. "You know I'm on a diet."

"You are always on a diet," I said to my stick-thin sister.

"Well, I have a date," she said, hugging my mom. "See you later."

"In the middle of the day?" I charged.

"The university is having a fund-raiser. And I'm helping Dan out."

"Who's Dan?" I asked.

"I can't keep them straight either," my mom said as Juliette flew out the back door.

"Are you taking those to the nursing home?" she asked. "Are they for Mr. Worthington? You might want to get it approved first. I think the residents there are on a strict diet."

"In that case, it sounds like Juliette is years ahead of her time," I said, and followed my sister out the door.

"So much for having my girls home," I heard my mom say as the door closed.

I wasn't sure where Brandon lived, but I did know someone who might. Even though it was winter, snowflakes and cold temperatures didn't keep the die-hard skaters from their outdoor skate.

I pulled into the lot and headed over to the ramps. Piles of snow lined the fences, but the ramps and rails were clear. Several skaters were flying down the half-pipe as if they were performing for a competition.

Hayley Phillips appeared as surprised to see me arrive as one could imagine.

"I didn't know you skated," she said. A few of the other skaters gathered around her.

I was only partially intimidated.

But it did look like fun. The skaters appeared as if nothing in the world mattered to them as each one sped down the ramps or did one-eighties at the top of them.

"Can you tell me where Brandon Maddox lives?" I asked. "It's around here somewhere and I figured you might know."

"Because we live in Riverside, you mean? We must all eat together and breed together?"

"No. Because I've seen you talking to him," I said in a nonconfrontational tone. "That's all."

"I didn't think your type would be seen in our parts," she said.

"I don't have a type."

"What's this about?"

"Something for school. Can you help me?" I asked sincerely.

Hayley popped her skateboard with her back foot and caught it with one hand.

"That was cool," I said.

Hayley wasn't softening or coughing up any information.

"Well, if you aren't all alike, then why would you think we are, too?" I asked. "I guess you might not be so different from the snobs you think I hang out with."

I began to leave.

"She was the one who had Nash invite Brandon to his party," I heard one of the other skaters say. "She's the one who stuck up for him."

"Hey—" Hayley called.

I heard the sound of a skateboard rolling up behind me.

"Follow this road to the stop sign," Hayley said. "Turn left. It's the third house on the right. It has a private drive."

I drove through Riverside and along a curvy side street. The homes were spread apart farther than on my street, with room for a few houses in between. When I saw a sign marked PRIVATE DRIVE, I knew it had to be Brandon's. Nervously, I turned into it. The tree-lined road was narrow and bumpy and passed a frozen pond. The front yard was several acres long. The modest-looking house appeared historic—likely built when the town was founded, but recently restored. The white paint glistened against the black shutters. Patches of gray shingles poked through the snow-covered roof. A six-foot metal windmill gently spun with the chilly wind. Several wooden snowmen welcomed guests. A white railing enclosed the front porch, and a wooden swing made it seem cozy. I was hoping to leave the package on the front porch and disappear before I was spotted.

I didn't plan on their dog. It barked so loudly from inside the house I thought it would alert all of Legend's Run. At first I thought it was a wolf snapping at me from the front window, but as I approached the door, I realized it was a husky.

I gingerly placed the package and card on the porch. I didn't dare knock, ring the bell, or holler. All I wanted to do was show my appreciation and run.

I tiptoed down the wooden steps. I snuck a look behind the house. There was land for miles. Between the front yard and the back, Brandon's family must have owned all of Riverside. There was a huge backyard leading to a tree-filled hilltop, bird feeders of every type, a small guesthouse, and Brandon's parked Jeep.

It was then I saw the sticker more closely. WWF—World *Wildlife* Fund—not World *Wrestling* Federation! Now I was truly embarrassed. Brandon liked animals in the wild, not the ones in the ring. What was I thinking?

The screen door squeaked opened. Brandon was trying to calm down his dog. I pretended not to notice and continued walking to my car when I heard the screen door close.

"Hey . . . Celeste?" Brandon called.

I did my best to pretend not to hear.

"Celeste!" he called again.

I had no choice but to turn around. It would have been rude not to.

Brandon caught up to me. He was handsome in his chestnut-colored thermal shirt and jeans. It appeared as if he'd been working in the house.

He held the tray of brownies in his hand. "What's this for?"

"I just wanted to officially thank you—for that day in the woods. But it's nothing really . . . just a small token."

"No—this is great." Brandon seemed so pleased with my gesture. "Thank you. Would you like to come in and have one?"

I wondered how many students Brandon had invited into his house since he'd arrived in Legend's Run. Were his grandparents home? Perhaps I was the first and only one to visit him. His house seemed so different from mine—with so much more character and charm. I was sure it was highly decorated on the inside, and I was more than curious to see how he lived. However, I wanted to exit the enormous property before Brandon saw my silly wrestling card.

"Thank you anyway. I really have to go."

"Always leaving me," he teased.

I couldn't help but break a smile. "I should be getting back home," I told him.

"You can at least wait until I open the card."

"That's okay—"

Before I could retreat, he was trying to slit the top of the envelope but was struggling with his wounded hand.

I took the envelope, opened it, and handed it back to him.

"Thanks," he said. His gaze lingered a bit on my face, then he read the card.

"Wow—this is so nice. You made it?"

I nodded, embarrassed.

"I don't think anyone has ever made me a card before. Thank you!"

I pointed to the bumper sticker on his car. "I thought it was for World *Wrestling* Federation," I confessed.

He laughed and then I did, too. There was something special about Brandon. His eyes were seductive.

There was a silence, and then I said, "Did you see a doctor?"

"Yes. I had to get stitches."

"I'm so sorry—"

"No—don't be sorry. That's not why I told you."

"I'll have to bake you more brownies now." We both laughed again.

"It's fine. Really," he said.

"That must have hurt."

"Nah," he said. "I'm a big boy."

"I'm sorry about Nash—that he gives you a hard time."

"Well, it's nice to have someone stick up for me, especially someone as pretty as you."

I blushed. So much so that I could feel my whole body redden.

"Wow—you have your own pond," I said. "You can go ice-skating."

He nodded, as if everyone had their own frozen pond. "Would you like to?"

"Like to what?"

"Skate? It's very shallow, so it's already frozen solid."

"You skate?" I asked quizzically.

"I played ice hockey at school. When I was growing up I came here during winter break and I got to practice. It was really cool."

"That does sound amazing."

"So, would you like to try?"

"I have plans this weekend. . . ."

"I mean now."

The thought of doing something spontaneously was unusual for me, to say the least.

"Now? I don't have any skates."

He sized up my boots.

"You might be able to use my grandmother's."

"She plays hockey?"

"No." He smiled. "But she has a pair of figure skates hanging on the wall."

"I wouldn't want to use her decoration."

"They aren't plastic. They're real. She used them herself. Besides, she'd insist."

Before I could say no, Brandon was on his way into his house. A few moments later, he came out with two pairs of skates.

Brandon handed me a tiny vintage pair of worn white dainty leather skates. His were in sharp contrast—sturdy, bold, and black.

He wiped off snow from the bench of the picnic table with his glove and offered me a seat. We sat down and removed our boots.

"I think these are a little big," I said, trying one on.

Brandon pulled my skate-wearing foot up onto his lap. "You just need to tighten them."

I loved how Brandon took charge—not in a bossy or controlling way but in a confident manner. I sat back as he tugged on the laces. I was mesmerized that he was being so attentive to me. "Now the other," he said.

"A girl could get used to this," I said. I continued to stare at him until he was finished.

It had been a few years since I'd put on a pair of skates. I was shaky when we stood, but Brandon handled himself like a pro.

"It's easy, just relax." He threw his other glove onto the table and extended his hand. I grasped it in mine. Even though I had stretchy gloves on, I could feel the power and warmth from his grip. I wobbled on the grass until we reached the frozen pond. I was a bit nervous, imagining myself lying flat on my back within seconds.

Brandon smiled and helped me onto the ice. It took me several moments to balance. "It's like riding a bike, right?" he said.

"Only on ice," I said.

"Yes, I guess there is that," he said.

"Now, let's go."

"We have to move, too?"

Brandon began to glide, taking me with him. My legs quaked underneath me. Brandon was as confident skating on frozen ice as he'd be if he was walking on the ground.

"You are thinking too much," he said. "Let your mind and body relax."

How could I not think? If I fell, I'd be smacking myself on a freezing pond, not to mention the embarrassment I'd feel in front of him.

"Here. Look into my eyes." He took both of my hands and we faced each other. I stared up into his warm and brilliant gaze as he began to slowly skate backward, pulling me forward.

My legs became like Jell-O and I clenched his hands. I wanted to take off my gloves so I could feel his skin against mine, but I was afraid he'd feel how nervous I really was.

"Now talk to me," he said.

"I have to talk, too?"

"Yes," he said. "What are your favorite things to do?" I still struggled to keep my gait relaxed; the more I tried the more I tensed up.

"Uh . . . I like to skate, but obviously I don't do it very often. I like to do things in the outdoors, but I really never get the chance to. So I mostly go to the mall, talk on the phone, hang with my friends."

"I see you writing in your notebooks. But you aren't taking notes. What are you writing?"

"Uh . . . nothing."

"It doesn't seem like nothing. You always seem very focused."

I couldn't tell him that I was writing down his name next to lips and hearts. I also couldn't tell him the other things I wrote for fear he'd laugh.

As we continued to skate, my legs relaxed and I began to gain confidence.

"So what are you writing?" he repeated.

"Just silliness. Stories and poems."

"What kind of stories?"

"One of the stories is about a guy who saves a girl from a pack of wolves."

"I hope it has a happy ending," he said.

"It does," I said.

"And what happens to the girl?"

"She becomes a nurse so she can help others."

"And the guy?"

"Well . . . he's bitten by the wolves," I said, thinking. "And it's underneath a full moon . . . so I suppose he could become a werewolf."

"Ah . . ." he said. "I like it. But couldn't he become a professional hockey player instead?"

I smiled. "Sure, I guess."

"And what happens to the guy *and* the girl?"

I didn't know what to say, but I knew what I *wanted* to say—that he falls in love with her. But what I wanted to say and what I could admit to him were very different things.

Just then my cell went off. It rang a funky ring. It was Ivy.

"You can get that," he said as we continued skating. He let my right hand go and I answered my phone.

"What are you doing?" my best friend asked.

If I said *holding hands with Brandon Maddox and skating on his pond*, she wouldn't believe me. Nor did I really want her to.

"You sound out of breath," she continued. "I'm on my way to pick you up."

"Uh . . . I'm not home," I said, alarmed.

Brandon and I continued to skate as I talked.

"Then where are you? I'll come get you." Ivy sounded impatient. "We have to work on our papers. You are the one who usually reminds me."

"Uh . . . give me a little while and I'll meet you at my house," I said.

"Fine, I'll see you there."

We hung up.

"You have to go?" Brandon asked with a hint of disappointment.

Neither one of us put on the brakes as we continued to coast around the pond.

"Not yet. What about you?" I asked. "Tell me something. Why did you move to Legend's Run?"

"My father was transferred to Europe, so I came here to stay with my grandparents."

"What does your father do?"

"He's a scientist."

"Wow—that is cool."

"Yes, it is, except when his job takes him out of the country."

"What about your mother?"

"She hasn't been in the picture for years."

My heart plummeted. I felt so sorry for Brandon, being without his mother and now his father.

"So your father is from Legend's Run?"

"Both of my parents are. My dad's parents stayed here, and I heard my mom's family all moved on. I really wouldn't know. Since my mom left years ago, we haven't kept in touch with her side."

He let go of my hands and skidded to a stop as I kept on gliding, alone. He watched like a handsome instructor proud of his pupil.

"It's okay—keep going," he encouraged.

I soaked up the crisp air. It felt good to be so free—of books, of cramped buses and crowded hallways, free from worrying about what my friends or Nash thought. The snow-covered trees were majestic. The birds flying in the overcast sky and the smell of smoke from the neighbors' fireplaces were invigorating.

It might have been just minutes of gliding, but to me it felt like hours. It was exhilarating to be skating solo and having Brandon watching me. I skated circles around the pond until I grew fatigued. Then I headed straight for him.

I used to know how to stop by spinning around. I decided to attempt it, but when I placed my blades at right angles, I spun off balance. I began to tumble and he caught me in his arms.

We laughed a deep laugh, so hard my stomach hurt. Brandon was so magnetic. I wasn't sure if he was going to kiss me, but I knew I wanted him to.

We locked eyes. He softly touched my frozen and flushed cheek. His hands were like a fiery stove, heating up my skin. He leaned into me and then my cell phone beeped with a text message.

"You are popular," he said, pulling away.

The mood was broken. I knew it would take courage for Brandon to kiss me. He saw me every day with the star of the football and basketball teams. He was new to school and already ostracized. The romantic moment was ruined.

I looked at the text message. "It's Ivy. She's almost at my house."

Reluctantly, we headed to the picnic tables and replaced our skates with our shoes.

"Hey, thanks for the brownies," he said, walking me to my car.

"Thanks for the skate." This was a moment when Brandon could kiss me. But his dog was barking, we were in plain view of his house, and I noticed a woman with brown hair peeking out from the front curtain. Then my cell phone rang again. I silenced it.

He opened the door for me. "Thanks for coming out to the sticks," he teased.

"This place is great," I assured him. "You have your own ice-skating rink. No one I know can say that."

As I drove off, Brandon stood by the driveway with two pairs of skates in his hand. I watched him, reflected in my rearview mirror, until I turned the corner away from his house and he was out of view.

THIRTEEN

full moon kiss

Brandon and I stole a few passing glances the next day at school but nothing more than that. I was dying to grab his hand when I saw him by his locker, like I had when we were skating, but I didn't possess the courage. Instead, I just daydreamed about him throughout each class and wrote his name in every one of my notebooks—in an out-of-the-way spot so my friends couldn't see. After school I was at Ivy's, working on our English essays, when my cell phone rang. It wasn't a ring tone I was familiar with—not Abby's, Nash's, or my parents'.

It was Frank Sinatra's voice singing "Fly Me to the Moon."

"Who is that?" Ivy asked.

Brandon's name appeared. How could that be? Then it

hit me; he must have added his name to my contact list when he found my phone in the woods.

I swept up the phone and covered it with my sleeve before Ivy had a chance to see it.

Frank kept singing.

"You better answer it and tell them they have the wrong number. Otherwise, they'll keep calling." My phone number was one digit off from a local radio station's. I'd been receiving calls from listeners requesting songs or dialing in for a contest, but I'd been too lazy to change my number.

I wanted to talk to Brandon so badly. I was dancing on the inside. I quickly answered before he hung up. "Hello?" I said.

"They're all gone," he said in a deep voice.

"What?" I asked.

"The brownies? They're all gone. Even the crumbs."

"Who is it?" Ivy asked.

"I think it's a wrong number," I whispered. The lie jumped out of my mouth before I had the chance to stop it.

"Only you'd answer them!" Ivy shouted. "Tell them they might have won if they dialed the right number for a change!"

"I'd like to give you back the pan. And your scarf," Brandon said.

I paused. What did that mean? A date?

"What are they asking?" Ivy asked.

"Or . . . I can sell them on eBay," he teased. "I'm sure they would get a lot since they belong to you."

I laughed.

"Why are you laughing at them? Are they requesting a song?" Ivy asked.

"Are you going to the game tonight?" Brandon asked.

"Yes," I said. "Are you?"

"Why are you asking *them* questions?" Ivy asked.

I imagined Brandon approaching me at the game with my mom's brownie pan and my scarf. The ref would whistle and the game would stop. The players and fans would leer in horror. Ivy and Abby would fold their arms in disgust.

"No, I have work to do," he finally said.

"You work?"

"Tell them to get back to their job before their boss notices they're listening to the radio instead of working," Ivy said. "You don't have to be so polite."

"There's a lot of upkeep around here and I help out my grandparents," he said.

Wow, I thought. That was kind of like when I volunteered at the nursing home. Brandon was putting his grandparents' needs in front of his own.

"But feel free to swing by here if you get a chance," he continued. "I'll be here."

I didn't say anything.

"If not, I'll get them to you later."

I didn't want to hang up. I wanted to talk to him forever. Even with Ivy in the room and my juggling antics, I was so happy to have Brandon on the phone. There was so much I wanted to know about him—so many things I couldn't ask now. And the one question that burned inside of me—what was it like to be kissed by him?

"I appreciate you calling," I finally said.

"Enough is enough." She grabbed the phone. "Would you like me to call your cell phone and request a song? Never call this number again."

She hung up the phone.

I was in shock.

"That's what you should have said from the beginning."

For the next few hours, I tried my best to focus on my essay about werewolves. But I couldn't help but let my thoughts wander to the wolves I'd met a few days ago, and how I was lucky even to be able to finish a complete sentence, all because of Brandon's heroic nature.

Since the Heidi Rosen fiasco at Nash's party, he and I were "off." However, that didn't keep my friends from dragging me to the basketball game and expecting reconciliation.

There were a lot of reasons to like Nash. He was handsome, athletic, and popular. He had enough money to do whatever a girl dreamed of—except he'd only do it if it was his dream, too. But instead of planning a possible reunion, my mind was focused on Brandon working at his house while all of us cheered for the Wolverines. I was so drawn to Brandon, I could think of nothing else.

"Maybe we should have a hockey team," I said to Ivy.

"We have enough problems raising funds to maintain football and basketball," she replied. "Now you want to build a hockey rink?"

"Not everyone likes those sports," I defended.

"Are you serious?" Ivy asked. "Who do you know in this town that doesn't?"

"Where did you get that idea?" Abby asked. "I'd like to play hockey. Only I'd want a pink uniform."

A few minutes later, Nash made a great three-point shot. The crowd rose to their feet and cheered, but I didn't budge.

"What's wrong with you tonight?" Abby said. "It's like you're not really here."

In fact, I was thinking about being somewhere else—somewhere that didn't have cheerleaders and screaming fans. Brandon's house wasn't too far away from school, and I figured it wouldn't hurt anyone if I just popped over and retrieved my things. I'd be back before the game was even over. My friends wouldn't miss me. The game was so riveting to them, it didn't matter who was sitting by them. Additionally, Brandon had wanted to return my items to me tonight, and if I hadn't already had plans, I might be there helping him out. Since Ivy hung up on Brandon, I was convinced he'd never call again. If I missed this chance, I wasn't sure I'd ever get another.

"I have to go," I said to Ivy.

"What do you mean? Nash is tearing up the court. You can't miss it!"

"I have to be somewhere."

"Where else could you be?"

"I'll be back soon. I promise."

Before she could say another word, I was gone.

I drove to Riverside. Normally, I was a pragmatic and practical person. Now I had to follow my heart. All I knew was that I needed to see Brandon and I couldn't fight it any longer.

This time I didn't need directions to Brandon's house. The first time I drove there, it was daylight. With a cloudy night and freezing temperatures, the full moon only shone every now and then. In Riverside there weren't streetlights illuminating the way, only white or yellow lines and reflective tape against the guardrails. I wasn't really used to these more rural roads, especially at night, and the trees were spooky when the headlights hit them. My heart began to race. What if I got a flat tire? How would I explain my location to my parents? And on this lonely road, would my family find me before a wayward stranger did?

As I pulled into the private drive, I got cold feet—what was I doing here to begin with? I shouldn't have left the comfort of my friends on the right side of town for the unknown adventures on the wrong one. At this moment, there was nothing to keep me at the gymnasium. Instead I was drawn toward Brandon.

My headlights shone on Brandon's Jeep.

Breathless, I knocked on the front door. The dog barked, but no one answered.

I ran to the back of the house. There was a small out-building the size of a two-car garage with a light shining from the window. I peered in, expecting it to be filled with tools, an old car, and a riding lawn mower. Instead there was a single bed, dresser, and TV. In the corner were a hockey stick and helmet and the pair of skates Brandon used yesterday. My scarf, pan, and card were sitting on the dresser. I felt warmth spread through me, knowing my things meant enough to him to have them displayed. I noticed some other things: a small wooden desk with a lit lamp and a laptop, a few bottles of medicine and bandages for his hand, stacks of books on wolves, deer, and other wild animals.

From the hilltop I could hear the faint sound of chopping. I followed the noise.

"Brandon?" I called.

I scaled the hill and was almost out of breath when I reached the top.

Brandon, in his brown leather jacket, was doing his best to chop wood. He struggled because of his wounded hand. He swore under his breath and shook out his hand in pain.

Then he caught sight of me. Startled, he jumped. "I didn't see you there," he said.

"I didn't mean to scare you."

"No—I'm glad you came."

"You hurt your hand again—"

"Oh—it's nothing. I'm really surprised to see you," he said. "I guess that scarf is really important to you. To leave the game . . ."

"Oh, yeah," I said. "The scarf."

"But you're wearing another one," he said, pointing to my green-and-white-striped one. "How many do you have?"

I didn't answer, I just stood nervously.

"I'll get your things for you. I just have to adjust this."

He stacked the broken pieces of wood with his good hand.

I didn't care about the scarf. I only cared about him. I wanted Brandon to touch me so badly and I wanted to touch him, too—to feel his embrace and lips against mine. I wasn't about to make the first move, and neither was he apparently. It wasn't my personality to be so romantically forward.

"Do you need help?" I finally asked.

"No, you sit down. It will just be a minute."

I sat on the chopping log.

Was he stalling so that I'd have to stay with him in the woods longer?

I rubbed my shoulder. If something didn't happen soon, I was going to scream.

"Is something wrong?" he asked.

"Just tension," I said.

"What do you have to be tense about?"

"Oh, everything, I guess. School. Tests. Boys."

"Boys?" he said. "Ah . . . that is stressful. Here, let me," he said, and came around behind me. "Your scarf is in the way. Do you mind?"

"Uh . . . no."

He peeled away my scarf and pressed his hand against my skin. My flesh tingled in his warm, strong hand. I was so in heaven, finally having Brandon being so close to me. Before I knew it, I felt his lips against my neck.

I was so overwhelmed I was afraid I'd fall off the chopping block and melt into the snow.

Suddenly Brandon stood in front of me and extended his good hand.

I stared up at him, his royal blue eyes shining down at me. I took his hand, stood, and he drew me close to him. Even through our heavy coats, I could feel the heat from our bodies pressed together. Overhead the clouds drifted apart, exposing a perfectly full moon.

The moon glimmered above us, magically illuminating us. When I'd looked at a moon like this before, it had always been when I'd felt alone— now it seemed to be smiling at me, as I was finally under its romantic glow.

I remembered Dr. Meadows warning me about the full moon. *Beware of a kiss under the full moon. It will change your life forever.* She had been right about the snow, the woods, howling, and an outsider. But what was the chance that she was correct about the rest? And what did it mean, really? I was so attracted to Brandon, I didn't know what to do.

"What? Is something wrong?" he asked.

"Oh, just something someone said. About the moon."

"It's beautiful, isn't it?"

"Yes, it is."

"Just like . . ."

He gently glided my hair away from my face.

"I've been wanting to do this since I first saw you," he said.

It was then he leaned into me and did what I'd been dying for him to do for so long. Since he first looked at me in Mrs. Clark's class, passed me in the hallways, and saved me in the woods. Brandon kissed me. His lips were so tender I thought I was in a dream.

It felt like nothing I'd ever experienced before. Deeper and more soulful than when I kissed Nash.

Something truly special had happened to me after seventeen years of living in Legend's Run. I'd fallen in love.

I began giggling with delight as Brandon wrapped his arms around me.

"What's so funny?" he asked.

"I don't know. I'm just so happy."

"I am, too."

I was in heaven in Brandon's strong arms. I didn't want to go back to the game. I didn't want this moment to ever end.

He caressed my cheek, and we kissed again so passionately I thought I'd gone to heaven.

I leaned my head against his chest and he stroked his

fingers through my hair. I could feel his heart pounding as fast as a bullet train. I gazed up and saw he wore a soft smile.

The full moon shone strong. He continued to stroke my hair and then kissed my neck and ears. My body tingled as his lips tickled my skin.

We kissed again, but suddenly he drew away.

"I don't have to leave," I said, referring to the game.

Brandon didn't answer. Instead, he released me from his embrace and stepped away.

"Really," I said. "I won't go. Not if you don't want me to. At least not yet."

"It's not that . . ." Brandon turned pale. "I feel odd."

"Maybe you should sit down," I said, pointing to the tree stump.

"No—it's something different. I feel really hot."

"That's because you are," I said, grinning.

"I'm burning up," he said, and took off his coat.

Our kisses had heated me up, too, but I wasn't ready to throw my coat to the side just yet.

Brandon ripped off his long-sleeved knit shirt and dropped it in the snow. He pulled off his undershirt and threw it at his feet. "I feel really weird," he said. "I'm not sure you should be around me. I think something's wrong."

I felt awful, too. We had just shared the best kiss of my life and now Brandon was acting strangely.

The fog from his warm breath seemed to be heavier and thicker than mine. I wasn't sure what was happening. "Maybe you've come down with something," I offered. "There's always some flu going around."

He kicked off his boots and yanked off his socks.

"What are you doing?" I asked.

But Brandon was far from focused on me. His brow furrowed and his gaze showed concern. This was no seduction.

He finally looked at me. Brandon was standing in thirty-degree weather in several inches of snow in just his jeans. He was barefoot and shirtless. And he wasn't shivering.

His chest was smooth and his arms were pale and lean. His chest heaved in and out rapidly.

"You must have a fever. But then you'd be shivering," I said, bewildered. "Let's go inside. Maybe your grandparents can help."

"No—they're not home. Besides, I don't think I should move."

Brandon started to shake. It was then I saw it. His royal blue eyes were a searing gray.

I couldn't believe my *own* eyes! I was stunned. How could his eyes change color? And why?

Now I began to shake. What was happening to Brandon? I was scared.

Brandon doubled over.

Maybe he did have the flu, but his symptoms were coming on so strong and so quickly, I wasn't sure what kind of flu it was.

Brandon pulled himself over to a tree and leaned his back

against it. I tried to follow, but he shooed me away. I wanted to respect his privacy, but I was really starting to worry. I cared for Brandon so deeply and was torn apart seeing him in distress. Since he wasn't going to leave the hilltop, I'd have to get someone to come to him.

"I'm calling the police. You need a doctor," I said.

Brandon didn't say a word.

The tree blocked my view of Brandon. It was dark except for the strong moonlight.

"Brandon," I said, "what's happening?"

"Please, Celeste. You have to leave." Brandon's voice was tormented and serious.

"No, I don't want to leave you."

"Please . . . go. Now!"

The more Brandon pushed me away, the more I wanted to stay.

"I'm calling nine-one-one," I said as a threat.

"Please leave, Celeste," he repeated. His voice was so deep, almost animal-like.

I kept hoping that at any moment Brandon would jump out and say "Gotcha!" like the millions of times Nash pranked me and our friends.

But he didn't and I was truly frightened.

"What are you doing?" I called. "You're scaring me! I'm going back to the game."

"Yes—that's . . . a great . . . idea." His voice was now shallow and breathless.

I retreated. I was torn. If this was a cruel joke, I didn't want to be its target. His brilliant blue eyes had changed to gray. It couldn't be possible. But if it was, then something was dreadfully wrong with Brandon and leaving him up there alone on the hilltop wasn't the responsible thing to do. He hadn't run away when I needed help. As scared as I was, I wasn't about to desert him in his time of crisis.

"I'm getting help," I called to him again.

He didn't answer.

Then he stepped out from behind the tree. Brandon's short, wavy brown hair was now savagely wild and shoulder-length. His normally clean-shaven face sported a goatee. His once-smooth chest was now lined with a thin layer of hair. His stomach was as ripped as an Olympic swimmer's, and his biceps were cut like a triathlete's. His eyes were a gorgeous gray. He was breathing heavy, as if he'd run a marathon. Brandon had fangs like a wolf.

I stopped dialing. I could barely breathe. It couldn't be . . .

Brandon continued to stare at me intensely, as if he wasn't sure what had just happened himself.

"Brandon! You look like a werewolf!"

His expression was sullen. He examined his arms and felt his stubble and goatee.

Brandon glared at me with the frailty of a human and the intensity of an animal.

I inched away. I was frightened and freaked out. Why was

he acting this way? A moment ago, I'd been on the other end of his irresistible lips. And now he was acting like a creature I'd never seen before.

I was afraid of him—of the situation—of being alone in the woods. The same person who'd saved me from a pack of wolves was now staring at me with their steady gray eyes.

Unsure of what he'd do next, I didn't break his mesmerizing gaze. I gently and quietly took a giant step backward. Unfortunately, my boot landed on a branch instead of solid ground. It cracked underneath my pressure, causing my foot to slip and I fell down.

When I looked up, Brandon was standing over me.

"No—" I cried, putting my hand out.

I was frightened and began to shake. He looked like he could rip me to shreds. But Brandon appeared confused by my fear. His intense expression softened as if he was as surprised as I was at his strange condition.

Suddenly he retreated into the shadows and disappeared.

In the distance, I heard a fierce howl, like that of a lone wolf.

sweet dreams

I didn't believe what I had just seen. Brandon turning into a werewolf? In the back of my mind, I kept thinking about the kiss. But how could that turn him into a werewolf? When he heroically saved me from the pack of wolves and was bitten, it was a full moon. But it couldn't be. . . . There had to be some rational explanation. Every magician had a secret, and Brandon must have had one, too.

Or perhaps I was dreaming.

I wasn't about to remain alone in the woods, in a dream or not, on the lonely hilltop by his house.

I grabbed Brandon's shirt and darted out of the woods. I ran as fast as I could to my car. I didn't look back until I was safely locked inside.

If this were truly a dream, then I wouldn't have Brandon's

shirt when I woke up in the morning. Unfortunately, that meant our magical kiss would have been a fantasy, too.

I was too shaken up to return to the basketball game. No amount of gossip or giggles with the girls could take my mind off of what I'd just witnessed or distract me from the most passionate kiss I'd ever had.

I managed to pull out of Brandon's driveway and onto the narrow road. With every turn and flash of my headlights in the lonely woods, I was terrified that some creature would jump out of the trees.

I tried to breathe slowly as I drove, convincing myself there had to be a rational explanation. It wasn't that Brandon had changed—it was me. The shadows of the moonlight distorted my view of his normally good-looking features and transformed them into wildly animalistic ones. Before we'd kissed, I'd distracted myself with thoughts of Dr. Meadows's prediction—*Beware of a kiss under the full moon. It will change your life forever*—and it toyed with my mind. And the other explanation—I'd been studying werewolves and it plagued my thoughts. How could I have seen him any other way? I'd been eating and breathing werewolf folklore, so it was only natural for it to have infiltrated my mind. The moon was full, we were in a darkened wood where wolves can lurk, and Brandon had been bitten. I'm sure I just mixed it all together, under the intoxication of finally having the kiss I'd been dying to receive. Maybe I'd felt guilty about my feelings for Brandon—and all the complications they would cause—and this was my way of projecting them.

But there was one thing that I couldn't explain away. The kiss. It was as magical as any transformation. Its power left an impact on me like a meteoroid hitting the earth.

I replayed the conversation I'd had with Dr. Meadows. She'd predicted all the events that happened—every decision that I made on my own—things that she had nothing to do with. But there was one thing she couldn't predict—me falling in love.

When I was safely home, I called and texted Brandon. But there was no response. As I paced in my room all night, my phone was silent. I dusted the dirt off of Brandon's shirt. It still smelled like him. I neatly folded it and put it on the nightstand. One thing was for sure: If I'd been dreaming, I'd know my werewolf essay was going to my head.

I awoke with a start. I'd just had the best dream ever. It was so clear. Brandon had kissed me in the woods behind his house. It was so passionate and intense it felt like it was happening now. I closed my eyes, not wanting to shake off the dream. I remembered more—Brandon took off his shirt, displaying his ripped chest . . . and then he began turning into a . . .

A wide smile and laughter overcame me. What a weird dream!

I sat up to find Brandon's shirt folded on my nightstand.

My breath escaped me.

The good news was that the heavenly kiss was real. I squeezed Brandon's shirt against me. The bad news . . . well, there had to be some real explanation for that. I told myself to just get up and go to school and try to figure this odd event out. As soon as I saw Brandon there, he'd secretly tell me what happened and we'd laugh off the whole thing.

I checked my phone to see if Brandon had tried to contact me. It was then I realized the time. Not only hadn't Brandon contacted me, but I'd overslept!

Why didn't anyone wake me? I bolted out of bed and shouted to my family.

When no one answered, I knew my parents had already left for work.

I quickly showered and dried my hair. I grabbed the first two items in my closet and got dressed. I didn't even have time to make sure they matched. I shoved Brandon's shirt into my backpack and took off.

I wasn't about to let anyone get in my way of finding Brandon and the answers to last night's events.

I managed to sneak into English class just as Mrs. Clark was handing back our graded homework. Brandon's desk was empty.

"Where have you been?" Ivy questioned me in the tone my mother usually takes. "Your clothes. Green shirt and orange sweater? You look like a pumpkin," she teased.

"Oh, this?" I asked, just now noticing my mismatched outfit. "I overslept."

"Well, I guess your fingerless-gloved friend did, too," she said. "Anything I should know about?"

For a moment I thought Ivy knew about last night. I shot her a look of horror.

"I'm just kidding," she said.

I was relieved, but only slightly. Brandon hadn't shown up for class. Since he attended Legend's Run High he'd never missed a day. I wondered what was keeping him away.

"You skipped the end of last night's game, too," she whispered. "Nash has been looking everywhere for you. He wants to make up."

For the entire period, my attention drifted to the closed classroom door. With each passing minute, it never opened. Where was Brandon? Was he still in the woods, at a hospital, or just home with the flu?

"So, where did you run off to so quickly last night?" Ivy interrogated me when she caught me staring vacantly at my locker. "Your lunch is *here*," she said, grabbing the sack off the top shelf. "What's with you? You are so not yourself."

"I had to do something at home," I said, shutting my locker. The two of us headed for the cafeteria.

"It couldn't wait?"

"Ivy," I began. I hadn't had a chance to talk to her privately since we'd arrived at school, and I wanted to tell her before the guys and Abby joined us. "Something happened last night," I confessed.

"Again? Did you encounter another wolf?"

"Yes, how did you know?" I was almost grateful that she might actually understand my strange predicament.

"Are you serious? I was just joking!"

"Oh," I said, deflated. "Well, truthfully, I think I did."

We reached the entrance to the cafeteria.

"Celeste. That's it. I'm not letting you out of my sight. Where were you? In your car?"

"No."

"In the woods again?" she asked, almost frustrated as we took our seats at our usual table.

"Well . . ."

Just then Abby arrived at the lunchroom with Dylan, Jake, and Nash.

Nash hung back, making it clear he wasn't along for the fun of it. He was as icy as Brandon's skating pond.

"I didn't see you in the stands last night," he said, taking a place at the opposite end of the table.

"I know. I had to leave," I said with indifference.

"So if you don't think it's important to stay at my games, how are we going to get back together?" he challenged.

It was our typical fight—he wanted me in the stands cheering him on at his practices and games. But there wasn't more to our relationship. We didn't have the same interests, and his always won out. It wasn't like he ever came to the nursing home and volunteered with me.

At the moment I had bigger issues to deal with than a

grumpy ex-boyfriend. "I—don't feel like talking about that again," I began.

"You should be kind to her." Ivy butted in. "She just ran into another wolf."

"A wolf?" Fear shot through his eyes. "Maybe if you stayed at the game the whole time," he said, "then you wouldn't be running into wild animals."

I was encountering wild animals, all right. I just wasn't sure how it had happened.

Beware of a kiss under the full moon. It will change your life forever. Dr. Meadows's words echoed in my mind. Not only had that moonlight kiss possibly transformed Brandon, but it had definitely transformed me. I wasn't adhering to my usual schedule, nor was I centered on studying, homework, and my friends. I wanted to know more about Brandon, where he was, and, most important, if what I saw last night was real.

But I wasn't getting any answers. Only heartache.

The moon looked full again tonight. Mr. Worthington was right. I jotted this revelation in the back of my notebook and began keeping a log of what I'd just experienced. The full moon. Brandon's bizarre behavior, his physical change, and how afterward I was riveted by this suddenly tormented soul.

The following two days Brandon wasn't at school. On the third day, when he didn't show for English class again, I was really starting to panic. I couldn't focus on our lesson, and when Mrs. Clark called on me, I was in another world. I really didn't know what was going on with Brandon or what to think. I hoped he wasn't sick. Then I feared he might have moved back to Miller's Glen. What had happened on the hilltop to change his appearance? Why couldn't he come to school?

I was zoned out on my way to my locker to get my lunch when someone yanked me into the crawl space underneath the main building's side stairwell.

Brandon was hanging on to me. He appeared frazzled and tired but as handsome as I'd ever seen him.

I could feel my whole body light up just being in his presence.

I wanted to hug him with all my might, but even though we were out of sight of passing students, I was afraid someone might see us.

"I wanted to talk to you about the other night," he said.

"Me, too. Are you okay? You haven't been to school for days."

"I know. I haven't been feeling well."

"Are you better now?"

"I think so . . . I'm not really sure. But about the other night. I want to know something."

"Yes."

"After we kissed . . . something happened."

"Yes, I know," I said sheepishly. "I was there."

"I'm sorry—" he began. "For anything that happened . . ."

"So it was a joke?" I asked. "I kept hoping it was."

I was relieved but totally embarrassed for getting so carried away with my paranormal thoughts and overactive imagination. I replayed my interpretations and feelings of the last few days. I started to laugh. I'd wasted so much time jumping to outlandish conclusions. I was so gullible.

"What do you mean?" he asked, almost confused. "You and me? You thought it was a joke?" His expression softened. It was as if I'd just insulted him.

"No. Not us." I melted inside. Brandon was so handsome standing before me in the secrecy of the stairwell. "I meant after."

"That's what I want to talk to you about. There's something I want to ask you," he said earnestly. "I got home and didn't have some items."

"What do you mean?" I pressed.

"My shirt. My shoes."

"I know. I have your shirt," I confessed.

"You do?"

"Yes. I kept it as proof." I showed him his folded shirt sandwiched in my bag.

"Proof?"

"That our time together wasn't a dream. I know . . . you must think I'm a dork."

"No—I think it's really cool." He smiled his gorgeous smile. "Speaking of dreams. I had a weird one that night."

"Yes?"

"When I woke up . . . I had dirt all over me. I just want to know . . . But I'm ashamed to tell you . . . Did we?" he asked in an honest and heartfelt tone.

Brandon wasn't referring to being a werewolf. He was referring to something else.

"No—" I assured him. "We didn't do anything like that."

"Really?" He was more disappointed than relieved.

"You really don't remember . . . anything?"

"Just us together under the moonlight. And that awesome kiss."

This time I smiled.

"But then I remember feeling weird. I think I might have had a fever and blacked out. I was hoping you'd tell me the rest."

I paused. "You really don't remember?" I repeated.

He shook his head.

"I'm not sure I can tell you the rest."

"Why not?"

"If I told you what I witnessed, you'd certainly think I was insane and never want to see me again." Besides, there was still the chance that I'd misinterpreted what I saw. There were no visible signs on Brandon that he was a werewolf. No scratches, no stubble, no wolflike fangs.

There had to be a third explanation. Brandon had a fever and the moonlight distorted my view of him. All I knew was that I couldn't wait until another moon to see him again.

"So, can you tell me what happened?" he asked sincerely.

"I'm not sure—"

"Of what?"

"That I really saw what I think I saw . . . and if I didn't, then you'll just think I'm crazy."

"How can I think that?" he asked. "You are popular, studious, and one of the kindest people I've ever met."

I swooned inside from his compliment.

"Because what I saw wasn't . . ." I trailed off.

"Wasn't what?" he pressed. Then suddenly he was concerned. "Did I hurt you?"

"No—of course not."

He sighed with relief. "Then don't you see—I can't remember. You have to tell me."

"I know you'll think I'm crazy—and you won't want to hang out again."

"But, Celeste, I want to see you. Again and again. Please tell me so tonight I won't continue to have weird dreams. I can dream about you instead."

I smiled. His words were like Cupid's arrow shooting through my heart. But I was still reluctant. I might lose Brandon—no more texting, calls, passing glances, or amorous kisses. But as Brandon gazed at me now, so worried and confused, tormented by not knowing what happened, I was torn. If he felt I was keeping something secret from him, maybe I had more to lose by not telling him.

"I need to know why I didn't have my shirt," he insisted. "Why I was covered in dirt. Why I dreamed I was a . . ." But he didn't finish.

I paused. Then I pulled him toward me so my lips were close to his ear.

"Because it looked like you turned into a werewolf." It slipped out in a whisper.

His suddenly sad blue eyes blazed through me. I was waiting for him to laugh or chew me out for being crazy. But he didn't do either.

The bell rang.

We lingered underneath the staircase, both shaken and confused. I didn't want to go to lunch and be apart from Brandon any longer, especially now, when I'd just revealed something so bizarre to him. I was hoping he would kiss me, but our secret romantic moment was ruined. The tapping of boots and the squeaking of sneakers on the vinyl floor were approaching us.

Suddenly the students began exiting through the stairwell, and we were both forced to leave separately.

sisterly advice

Winter break was usually one of my favorite times of the year. Not only did everyone in town decorate their houses with festive, twinkling lights and their yards with snowmen, penguins, and reindeer, but it meant two weeks of vacation. Free time to do whatever I wanted. And Ivy, Abby, and I had sleepovers, all-night gabfests, and endless laughs. I could sleep in as long as I'd like to and be my own boss.

But this year, winter break was torture. It meant two torturous weeks without seeing the guy who had stolen my heart. Practically every moment was spent thinking about him—him saving me, the first time I held his wounded hand in mine, the kiss of a lifetime. And when I wasn't dreaming about him, I was worrying about him and the strange condition I found him in underneath the full moon. Instead of relishing my days of freedom, I longed for the ringing of first bell and the start of English class. But winter break crept along without him, monotonously.

I continued to wonder if what I saw that night was real and agonized over how I'd handled the situation. If I had to give advice to the lovelorn about what to say when seeing a guy again after sharing a spectacular kiss and hoping for another date, it would be to say one of these three things: "Had a blast," "I hope we can hang out again," or "Here's my number." The one thing I'd never advise saying would be, "It looked like you turned into a werewolf!"

How did I expect Brandon ever to call, text, or contact me when I'd told him that?

I was so confused about my feelings toward Brandon. Maybe it was time to turn back and not continue down this uncharted road I'd been traveling on. When Nash returned from vacation with his parents, it would be my chance to reconcile with him, put all this Westsider fascination to rest, and move on in the direction my life had already been taking. But I cared for Brandon so deeply, it just wasn't something I had control over. And I assumed Brandon was mixed up as well. He was the one going through something—strange dreams, not remembering the nights, and missing school. If I contacted him, I'd only be adding to his already suddenly complicated life.

Having Juliette home during the break only added to my angst. She was in and out of our front door with different guys, laughing and giggling and staying out until the wee hours. All I wanted to do was see one guy, be near him, touch him, and kiss him. My skin hurt without Brandon's touch, my mind raced with thoughts of him. I realized there was only one person I could turn to in my time of need, who knew more about love, romance, and hot guys than anyone I'd known—someone who might have the answers for my obsessive romantic feelings and how to cure them.

I knocked on my sister's bedroom door. When she didn't respond, I opened it to find her putting the final touches on her makeup.

"Don't you knock? I could have been undressed," she argued.

"But I did knock, and you aren't undressed."

"Well, I could have been."

Juliette was so pretty she didn't need to wear makeup. But still she spent endless hours in front of the mirror painting her face with whatever colors were in that particular season.

Juliette's room was in stark contrast to my own. Mine was filled with books, DVDs, and trinkets. Where other teens had band or movie posters hanging on their walls, my sister had framed pictures of herself with her friends and various boyfriends.

"Jules, I need to ask you something," I said, sitting on her bed. "How do you know if you are in love?" I asked, fiddling with the frame on her nightstand.

"You'll know."

I sighed. I didn't want a vague answer that I could get from anyone. I wanted someone to speak to me about specifics.

"Why, are you in love with Nash?" she asked. "He is really hot." Juliette turned away from her mirror and toward me. "Is he trying to pressure you?"

Nash always wanted more from our relationship than I was prepared to give. But that wasn't it.

"No—it's not *that*," I said.

"Because if he is, I know some guys in my dorm who will make him wish he hadn't."

"No—"

"Don't you do anything you're not ready to do. You understand? That is the most important thing. Only when you are ready and only when you're much older."

Now she was lecturing me. But I didn't mind. Almost. It was sweet that she cared about my well-being.

"He knows where he stands with me," I said. "Anyway, I'm talking about love."

"With someone else?"

I nodded.

"Does Nash know?"

"No, of course not. Besides, we aren't seeing each other right now."

"Great. What did he do now?"

"It's no biggie."

"Are you sure?"

"Yes."

"Good. Then let's talk about the new guy! Have you gone out on a date?"

"No."

"So, it's a crush from afar?"

"Well. . . . not really . . ."

"Then what is it?" she asked impatiently.

"I met him at his house. We went ice-skating."

"I'd call that a date."

"You would?"

"Yes! Did he kiss you?" she asked.

"No. Not then . . ."

"You've kissed him?"

When I didn't answer, she put down her makeup and hopped on the bed.

"You kissed him?"

"Accidentally," I said. "I didn't mean for it to happen."

"That's the best kind."

"I mean I was waiting, like forever. But then it just happened!"

"I love it!" My sister high-fived me.

I couldn't rein in my smile if I'd had Botox. I hadn't told anyone, so it was good to finally girl-talk with someone. Even if it was my sister.

"What was it like?"

I was too embarrassed to talk about it.

"C'mon! Tell me."

"It was heaven. Amazing. Like nothing I've ever felt in my life."

She squealed with delight. Suddenly we were reduced to two giggling girls.

"So who is this dreamy guy who's stolen my little sister's heart?" she asked. "I want names and dates. What does he look like?"

I didn't say anything.

"Describe!" she ordered, pointing her mascara brush at me.

"Brown wavy hair, royal blue eyes. His lips are full and dreamy. His stare can penetrate your soul."

"Wow! Can you introduce him to *me*?"

"He's in high school!"

"Does he have a brother?"

"I don't know . . ."

"Does he have a name?" My sister was getting frustrated.

"I'm not giving you names."

"Okay. Okay."

"Uh, you wouldn't know him. Besides, I'm not sure if it's love or the flu," I said.

"What are your symptoms?"

"Come on . . ."

"Symptoms!" she demanded.

"All right. I can't eat. I can't sleep. I can't focus on school or even the most menial tasks. And I'm obsessed with thinking about him."

"That's love. Or at the very least lust. Something I prefer."

I sighed. "Do you think these feelings could distort my view of him?"

"What do you mean?"

"Physically. Like the way he looks."

"Of course. Some girls fall for the lamest guys but think they're studs 'cause they are clouded by love."

"But like . . . could these feelings make him look more muscular? Grow a goatee?"

"Guys can get stubble by the end of the day. That's normal."

I mean instantly, I wanted to say.

"And make his hair appear longer and his eyes change color?" I asked hesitantly.

"If you mean going from blue eyes to twinkling liquid blue eyes, then yes, that can be because you're love-struck. But if you're talking about blue eyes changing to brown, then no."

My smile turned into a frown. I grew worried.

"What are you getting at?" she asked.

"Oh . . . nothing."

"Love can distort your view of him," she said, patting my leg. She obviously didn't know that I was alluding to him becoming a lycan, but I appreciated my sister's reassurance.

"When did you first fall in love?" I asked. "Was it with Brad or Jason?"

"Are you kidding?" she asked with a laugh. "No," she said as if I must have already known. "I've never been in love."

I was floored. My sister had had a guy on her arm since kindergarten. How could she not have fallen in love by now? I felt sad that I may have actually experienced the feelings of true love before she had. With all the guys she dated, not one had penetrated her materialistic heart? Of course, we were still young and she had her whole life ahead of her, but I'd figured she'd been in love countless times. That just reinforced for me that I couldn't ignore the feelings that I had for Brandon—that they were as real as the shirt I had sitting on my nightstand.

"Are we finished with our chat?" she asked, packing up her makeup.

"Almost. I'm doing a research paper on folklore. It's about werewolves."

"You would pick the creepy stuff. Why didn't you pick fairies? I still have my paper somewhere. You could have used mine."

"You know there's a legend here about werewolves?" I asked.

"Yes, I've heard," she said, as if I thought she was an alien.

"Do you think the legend is true?"

"Do I think there really are werewolves lurking in the woods of Legend's Run, showing their scruffy faces under the full moon? Attacking animals and carrying off women, never to return? It does sound romantic in a weird way."

"Yes, it does," I said, thinking.

"We always imagine what we can't understand. Like love."

"But love can be real. So does that mean werewolves can be, too?"

"I'm sure people see things in the dark and then just put a face on it," she surmised.

"But you're not answering my question," I said impatiently. "Do you believe in werewolves?"

"No."

It was that simple. My sister didn't believe in werewolves. And even though I thought I might have seen one, I didn't believe in them either. At the end of the day, we had that much in common.

SIXTEEN

moonlit stroll

I was buzzing when I returned to school after winter break. Hoping to get to English early, I raced to my locker, where I found a single pink rose sticking through the metal handle.

I was so truly touched, I tingled all over.

"Isn't that sweet?" Ivy said. "Nash is saying he's sorry."

"Nash?" I asked, bewildered.

It hadn't occurred to me that it was from Nash.

"Uh . . . yes, it is, I guess." I was grateful to receive a flower from anyone—but I was disappointed that it wasn't from Brandon.

"You guess?" she asked. "He's apologizing. Maybe you should accept it already."

I held the rose in my hand and leaned against the locker.

It would be so easy and I knew I should consider myself

lucky to go out with Nash. He was gorgeous by anyone's standards, and a gifted athlete. It would be so simple for the "six clique" to hang out together. But something happened to me when I saw Brandon that day in English class and our eyes met. The unbelievable heroism that he displayed in the woods was hard to dismiss. And even more so was the most passionate kiss of my life. My life had been pretty easy—or rather ordinary. Go to school, study, hang with my friends, volunteer. Now I was putting everything on the line for a guy who I barely knew—who might indeed have some kind of paranormal powers. But I felt this misunderstood new student filled in so many places that had been empty in my heart.

"Nash could date any cheerleader he wants," Ivy said. "But he likes you because you aren't that typical girl. It's you he keeps coming back to."

"Well, now I'm not so sure that's a good idea."

"I don't want to hear it," Ivy said. She liked the status quo—everything as it should be—Abby and Dylan, Ivy and Jake, and Nash and me. Six best friends who would hang out together, go to the same colleges, and eventually get married.

I didn't want to be the one who broke up my best friend's plans. But I wasn't sure if Ivy's dream should come at the expense of my happiness.

After school, I was heading toward the parking lot to meet Ivy, my rose poking out of my backpack.

"Hey, what's up?" Nash asked, catching up to me by the

flagpole. He looked handsome and tanned from his holiday break at the beach.

I could see Brandon in the distance, opening his Jeep door. He paused.

"Thanks for the flower," I said. "It was really sweet of you."

"The flower?"

"Yes, the one sticking out of my locker." I took it out of my backpack and showed him.

"Oh, yeah, that one," he said. "I have so much on my mind lately. Jet lag and all."

I was slightly heartbroken. I was really hoping it was from Brandon.

"Aren't you going to thank me for it?" he asked.

Now I paused. Brandon was watching me. There was no way I was going to kiss Nash, even for the kind gesture of a flower. I should still be miffed at him for his behavior at the party—having Heidi Rosen's legs on his—but I wasn't. I didn't want to kiss him because I wanted to kiss Brandon instead.

I gave Nash a quick hug, but he held on longer than I wanted or expected.

"I was hoping for more," he said, stroking my hair.

"Maybe later," I said, breaking away.

"So, now we're back together?"

I heard a car door slam in the distance. The Jeep tore out of the parking lot.

"Not yet," I said, and headed off to join Ivy and Abby, who were just exiting the gymnasium.

When I got home, I headed into Juliette's room. Rolling suitcases, totes, and duffel bags, all busting at the seams, were scattered on the floor. She was digging in her closet, making last-minute grabs at shoes and clothes for her return to college.

"Here, you can have this," I said flatly, placing the flower on top of her suitcase.

I headed to my room as a beep sounded from my phone. It was a text from Brandon.

You thanked the wrong guy, was all it said.

I raced back to Juliette's and grabbed the flower.

"I thought that was for me—" she said, confused.

It was from Brandon after all. I danced around my room until I was so dizzy I collapsed onto my bed. I clutched the flower to my chest and held it as if it were him.

"You're crazy!" I heard my sister call. "No wonder you don't have a normal love life!"

I raced over to Brandon's as fast as I could while still maintaining the speed limit and avoiding darting animals crossing the road. I wasn't sure if Brandon was home or not and didn't want to text or call. I just wanted to see him. Besides, the moon was waning and would not be full for a couple of weeks. If he *was* a werewolf, we both were safe.

I drove past the Maddoxes' frozen pond and toward his

place. Brandon was shoveling snow outside the guesthouse when he saw my car approaching.

He looked pleasantly surprised to see me, but reluctant, too. I could tell he wasn't sure how I'd react to him since we hadn't seen each other since our encounter underneath the school's staircase.

"Thank you for the flower," I said, meeting him by the fence. "I wasn't sure it was from you."

"Seems you were thanking the wrong guy."

"I know," I said, feeling stupid. "I thought it was from—"

"I should have left you a note. I just thought if it got in the wrong hands, your friends might freak out."

I hated that Brandon knew my predicament. If they were real friends, one could say, it wouldn't matter to them who I dated just as long as I was happy. But my friends wanted us to be cozy in our perfect sixsome—three best girlfriends dating three best boyfriends.

I lingered by the fence near Brandon. It was as if he, too, longed for us to be together but, like me, was acting cautiously.

He leaned over and said, "I didn't know how you'd react to getting a flower from a werewolf."

"I'm so sorry I called you that," I said. "I didn't mean—"

"That night—it was strange," he admitted. "I still don't know what to make of it."

"You still don't remember?"

"I remember the way the moonlight lit your face and eyes. I can't get it out of my mind."

My cheeks flushed red. "And after? You remember now?"

He shook his head. "I know something happened. It changed me. Although I'm not sure how or why, I know it did." Then he leaned on the fence, his hair falling over his eyes. "I wanted you to know that I was thinking of you. I've just been trying to figure some things out."

"I understand," I said.

"You do?"

"Something extraordinary did happen that night. We both felt it."

I could sense his sudden relief with my reassurance.

"Have you told anyone about that night?" he asked, concerned that I'd spread what I told him around school.

I'd told Juliette vaguely, but not the real details and who the juicy kiss was with. "You don't have to worry about that," I said. "No one knows."

"Well, I'm glad you are here, now," he said. He took my hand. "I was hoping I could take you on a proper date sometime."

I nodded enthusiastically. "I'd like that."

Dates with Nash were always set around his sporting events. I was eager to find out what Brandon's idea for an evening out might be. Although, Brandon was so charming that as long as I was with him, I didn't care where we were.

"Are you cold?" he finally asked. "We can go inside—"

"No, it's not too bad." I liked being with Brandon. I admired him for knowing so much about the wilderness. I wanted to share it all with him—the snow, the bare trees, the cold, crisp air.

"You like the outdoors?" he asked.

"Yes."

"Back in Miller's Glen my friends liked to hang inside and party. Like the Eastsiders here."

"You mean you were on the Eastside?"

"Every town has their Northside or Southside . . . east or west. Every side thinks they are better than the other. It's all a waste of time."

"So you mean you were on the popular side in Miller's Glen but not here?"

"Funny, isn't it? No one here would know. I'm just a Westsider to them. That's why you are so cool," he said.

"I bet you miss your friends," I said.

"I do. But they weren't really into outdoor stuff. That's why I like it here so much. We have so much land and so much to do."

"You like it here?"

"Yes. My grandparents are really awesome. They're funny and sweet. My grandma is always stuffing me with food. I get this cool bachelor pad guesthouse and this backyard and a pond where I can practice hockey."

"Is that different from your house in Miller's Glen?"

"Totally. I lived in the suburbs. We had a backyard, but not like this. It had a grill and a few patio chairs. Nothing unusual."

"What about school?" I hinted. "I bet it's hard to transfer to a new one, especially after it already began."

"I don't think about it much. I like certain classes," he said. "The ones I have with you."

I could hang out with Brandon forever, but I longed to touch, hold, or kiss him. It had been torture this last month and I couldn't stand it anymore.

It was then he took my hand. I sighed inside. We walked around his property holding hands.

"That night, something strange did happen," he said. "I haven't felt the same since."

"Neither have I."

"I've never met anyone like you."

"Me, too."

"But since that night, I haven't slept well."

"How did you feel during winter break?" I asked, trying to pull more info from him.

"I dream a lot. During the day I feel great, but I'm ravenous. My grandmother says she can't keep up with my meals for lunch and dinner. She has to go to the grocery almost every day."

"What did you dream about?"

"Just stuff. The woods," he said. "I think it's because I'm

sleeping out here in the guesthouse. Noises in the night must be infiltrating my subconscious."

Brandon was obviously tormented by what he was going through. He fingered his hair and stared off into the hilltop.

"I'm so sorry—I want to help you."

"Don't worry," he said. "After that night I felt weird for a few days. Bizarre dreams and waking up without my shirt and covered in dirt. I think it was just a fever. Since then, I just have weird dreams and the events of the night are fuzzy, but when I wake up I feel okay, and I'm fully clothed."

He obviously could see the concern on my face. "I feel much better, now that you are here."

The sun was setting behind the trees.

But I was distracted. The moon was crescent-shaped, framed by puffy clouds. If Brandon was indeed affected by the wolf's bite, and Mr. Worthington's story about the full moon was real, then we were safe from the crescent moon's glow. For now.

"What are you looking at?" he asked.

"The moon."

"It's beautiful, isn't it? I like it when there is that spooky glow around it. But I'd rather be looking at something else right now."

Brandon moved close to me, so close, it took my breath away. He pulled me into him. We were standing face-to-face, our fingers entwined. He leaned into me and kissed me with such desire and intensity I thought I was dreaming.

But like all good dreams, it had to come to an end, because the next thought in my head was that our romance would have to stay a secret. And I'd have to find out if what I'd seen after our first kiss under the full moon meant that Brandon Maddox was, in fact, a werewolf.

SEVENTEEN

so many secrets

For as long as I could remember, I hadn't kept anything a secret from Ivy. Half the time it was because she squeezed information out of me, the other half because I blurted it out in excitement. Now I had been keeping several major events under wraps for quite some time. Besides discreetly seeing Brandon, I'd managed to keep three classified secrets: one, that Brandon Maddox had rescued me from the wolves; two, that I was in love with him; and three, the Westsider I was in love with might possibly be a werewolf.

The secrets burned inside me. If I told Ivy about Brandon, she'd be upset that I was in love with anyone other than Nash. And if I told her he might be a werewolf, she'd clearly think it was a prank. She'd be in as much disbelief as I had been and, like me, would want proof. Finally, the news of a teen werewolf would spread through the town faster than a flood. Brandon's existence would ultimately be at stake. Before I told anyone anything, I needed to know for sure what was happening with Brandon—if his dreams and what I thought I'd seen meant that he was, indeed, a werewolf.

My calendar and my notebook became my best tools. As the days passed by, I logged all possible lycanthropic events—the three nights when the moon appeared full, Brandon woke up shirtless and covered in dirt. Brandon dreamed a lot during waning and waxing moons. He was ravenous during the day. And I noted the shapes of the moon and circled the date of the next full moon, which was several weeks away.

Brandon continued to be a loner at school—keeping to himself in the cafeteria while my friends and I gathered at the popular table. I was completely torn up about it. I wanted to go over and sit by his side. Every other table was crowded with friends and cliques. I'd be the only one to break out of the pattern that had gone on for years in Legend's Run. Most important, I would lose my best friends if I chose the Westside over the East. Plus, I worried that Brandon could change his mind about me at any moment. He clearly had some strange things going on in his life. But I couldn't get his kisses out of my mind, and of course, his saving me that day in the snow created a special bond between us.

Regardless, I watched Ivy and Abby chat and cuddle with their boyfriends as day after day I'd stare at Brandon and watch him eat alone, all the while wanting to be sitting beside him.

"Why so glum?" Ivy asked one day at lunch.

"It's nothing."

"You miss Nash, don't you?"

"Now that you mention it . . . I—"

"You do?" she said.

I don't, I was going to say. "Why don't we invite Brandon to sit at our table?" I asked Ivy. I gestured to the handsome guy, who was pulling several über-sandwiches from his bag. "He eats by himself every day since he moved here."

"Are you kidding?" Abby asked. "He's a pig. Look at him eating. He has three sandwiches. If you sat next to him, he might take a chunk out of you, too." My friends laughed.

"I just thought it would be nice to include him," I said.

"Maybe there's a reason he doesn't have friends," Abby said, tapping my shoulder.

I sighed. I didn't know how I'd ever be able to make my friends accept the boy I was secretly in love with.

Nash had been on his best behavior toward me. Though I resisted, he insisted on escorting me to my classes and on buying me lunch every day. I wasn't used to all this attention from him. Nash was turning into the boyfriend he should have been all along. However, I kept him at bay. I never kissed him or in any way considered a rekindling of romance.

The odd thing was that the more aloof I became toward Nash, the more he tried to win me back. Nash was like a wolf in the wild—his territory was being invaded and he was here to reclaim it. If I had been doting on him like I had in the past, I was sure he'd probably ignore me the way he had when we were dating. Whether Nash knew it or not, he was feeling the effects of my admiration for Brandon.

But I suffered in silence. Brandon's shirt was my only reminder of our night together and that kiss under the full moon. I imagined his turmoil dealing with a condition that he hadn't asked for.

Brandon was elusive again, as he had been in those days and nights following the full moon about three weeks ago. He was often late for class and then snuck out before I could catch up to him. He might have been protecting me from himself, or maybe he was finally blaming me for causing his condition. I showed up at his house, and even walked around his hilltop. But my calls to him went unanswered.

One day in study hall I began to cut off the tips of my knit gloves and tried my fingerless gloves on.

"What are you doing?" Ivy asked.

"I thought it would be cool to wear them like this," I said. "This way I can keep warm and use the computer or write my essay."

"You do think of everything," she said. "But I warn you, it does look a bit Riverside."

That was exactly the look I was hoping for. My new fashion statement was the only way I could show Brandon my solidarity and let him know I still was thinking of him. I wanted to slip him notes in his locker, but it was too risky and I wasn't that brave.

I'd caused his lycanthropic condition, and the amount of guilt I felt was enormous.

"Mr. Maddox, we'll have to speak after class," Mrs. Clark said one day in English when Brandon showed up a half hour late.

"I told you he was juvie," Ivy whispered. "And to think we invited him to Nash's house for the party."

"We didn't," Abby said. "Mother Teresa did."

"I know you are kind," Ivy said, "but you have to be careful. You can't bring in every stray cat you see. Some of them have fleas, you know."

"Brandon isn't like that," I said.

"How do you know?" Ivy asked.

"Yes," Abby pressed. "How do you know?"

"Look at him. He's . . ." I began.

"Yes?" Ivy said.

"He's clean. He takes care of himself," I said.

"Are we looking at the same guy?" Ivy asked.

Brandon looked exhausted. He kept his coat on all day and barely stayed awake through class. It was apparent to me that the dreams he was having were taking a toll on his body.

"He's probably doing drugs," Abby said.

"He is not!" I defended.

"How do you know?" Ivy wondered.

"I just don't think we should rush to judgment," I said.

"But that's what we do," Abby said. She and Ivy laughed.

"There are signs," Ivy said. "He has bags under his eyes. He keeps his hands covered. He's troubled. This isn't a pound. You can't take care of everyone. You might have to let this one go."

"Besides, you have this hottie waiting for you tonight," Abby said.

"Ladies," Mrs. Clark reprimanded. "Time to pay attention."

Were my friends right? Was I choosing the wrong course? I was always the rational one in our clique—daydreaming and caring, but terminally practical. Though I dreamed of becoming a writer, I really wanted to be a nurse or a doctor. I wanted to help people and have a career that could be stable. But now nothing seemed stable. If I followed my head, I'd get back together with Nash. Not only would I be making the rational choice, but I'd be making my best friends happy. However, if I followed my heart, I was on an uncharted course with conditions possibly unfavorable.

After English, Mrs. Clark asked to see Brandon. Ivy, Abby, and Nash went on to their next classes while I stalled, straightening the contents of my locker.

I hadn't been able to catch Brandon for days, so this was my only chance.

"Brandon," I said when he finally came out of the classroom.

He held a slip of paper. It must have been a detention.

"You can't run away from me here, too," I said.

"I'm not running away from you," he said sincerely. "It's just it might be best—"

I couldn't bear to hear him finish his sentence. "It's my fault," I said. When no other students were around, I pulled him into the crawl space of a vacant stairwell.

"Of course it's your fault," he said.

I was hurt. Brandon did blame me—though he was right to do so.

"Yes," he continued. "I'm restless. Can't concentrate. You're not going to make me say any more, are you?" He grinned. He was wickedly handsome, and I was flattered by his romantic implication.

"Then why won't you see me?" I asked him.

He took my hand. He laughed at my gloves, as they were just like the ones he was wearing. "I just haven't been myself, and I thought it best if I didn't complicate your life. I'm still having these strange dreams," he continued. "It's probably because I've had to make a lot of adjustments to a new school. That's what Mrs. Clark said."

"I thought she gave you a detention."

"No, it's a slip to see the school shrink. I keep having these bizarre dreams," he confided. "I wake up exhausted, or I oversleep."

"Are you waking up in the same condition you were in when you went to sleep?"

"I think so. My memories are still fuzzy, but it's not like those times after we first kissed and I woke up . . . like I'd slept out in the woods."

"What are the dreams about?" I asked.

"You'll laugh. That's why I haven't told you—"

"You have to tell me." I was adamant this time.

He paused. "It was like the one I had after we met on the hilltop. When I wake up I only remember bits and pieces. But by the time I'm out of bed, I forget it. I only remember brief images."

"What do you remember?"

"It's the same every night. I'm a wolf. Only when I run, I run like a man."

He waited for my reaction.

"See—I knew you'd think I was crazy!" he said.

"No—it's just that—" I began. "I'm afraid, too. To tell you the truth."

"I'm not sure I want to hear it, but I think I know it."

"Those first few nights—when the moon was full— those weren't dreams, Brandon."

He was startled and let go of my hand.

"I was there," I said. "I saw it happen."

"Then for the next couple of days—you said you woke up, and you didn't come to school. Those were the days the moon appeared full. Then the moon waned and you don't turn, but you continue to dream as if you are."

"It's not real, Celeste. It can't be—I won't allow—"

It was hard enough to prove Brandon's transformation really happened and convince myself it was real. But for Brandon to accept his new fate could be devastating. Mrs. Clark was right. He should see the school counselor.

Brandon shook his head as if he was shaking the truth away from him.

"But you are so gorgeous and powerful," I tried to convince him.

"But if I don't remember, then it can't be real? Right?"

"Maybe it's best you don't remember. Until we get you help."

Brandon choked out the words: "What if I'm a monster?"

"You aren't. You're just stronger and more handsome . . . if you can believe that."

"How do you know, Celeste?"

"I was with you."

"The whole night?"

"Uh . . . no."

"So how do you know who I am or what I do when you're not there?" Brandon's torment was palpable.

I put my arms around him. At this point, I didn't care who saw us together. "Uh . . . I don't. But—"

"Then neither one of us really knows, do we? How did this happen?" he asked. "How did this ever happen?"

"It's my fault," I blurted out. "I tried to tell you before. I was warned about the full moon . . . about the woods and the wolves . . . about the kiss. And now the moon, full or not, causes your nocturnal affliction or your bizarre dreams. It's my fault this happened to you. If you hadn't been bitten by that wolf. If we hadn't kissed under the full moon. If I'd listened—"

"Celeste, promise me something."

"Anything." This was the moment that Brandon might be asking me to be his girlfriend—to stick by him while he went through his ordeal. He'd want me to bravely confront my friends and make our relationship public so I could finally support him the way he ought to have been supported all along.

He took a breath and stared deeply into my eyes. "Tomorrow is a full moon. Promise me that you won't see me anymore."

It was as if I'd just found out I'd failed every class I'd ever taken. I was devastated at the news. "I can't!" I said. "I won't."

"At least until I have this figured out," he said sadly, cupping my face in his hands. "I understand if you won't wait . . . but you can't contact me, Celeste. Don't you understand? You can't—"

"I know you. You wouldn't do anything to hurt anyone."

"I want to be with you, more than you know. It's just at night . . . it's best that you aren't around me."

My heart broke. I'd finally fallen in love, and I wasn't able to be with the one person I'd fallen in love with. I felt as if he were being shipped off to an overseas boarding school never to return. But Brandon was here—in my classes, the hallway, and the lunchroom. He wasn't saying we couldn't see each other because he didn't care for me. He was saying it because he cared.

I didn't want Brandon to leave our secluded spot underneath the staircase. I was afraid I'd never be able to be with him again. He must have felt the same thing because this time he took a chance he hadn't taken before. He drew me into him and gave me the most heartfelt kiss. It hit me through my heart and down through to the soles of my shoes.

It was as if he was saying good-bye.

Brandon disappeared into the hallway as I sat down and sobbed.

I didn't have anyone to talk about my problem with—no school shrink would have the answers. No one would understand. No person could help. No soul would believe me.

Or was there someone who would?

EIGHTEEN

the doctor is in

Out of breath, I arrived at Penny for Your Thoughts to find the shop dark and a hanging sign with the word CLOSED.

I wondered if Dr. Meadows was sequestered in her back room giving another clichéd reading like she had given to my friends. Or was she giving one like mine—dead-on?

Whatever she was telling her client, it couldn't be more important than what I had to tell her. I knocked until my hand hurt.

A man the size of several normal fathers combined, with a shaved head and more tattoos than skin, lumbered out from the store next to Penny for Your Thoughts.

"She's closed today. Can't you read the sign?"

"Uh . . . yes. It was just that sometimes she puts the sign

out when she's doing a reading."

"This is her day to stay at home."

The man could have easy squashed me like a bug. Normally, I would have gotten back in my car and given way to the large, tattooed obstacle obstructing my goal. But Brandon's life was on the line and I had to drum up all my courage to get to Dr. Meadows.

"Do you know where she lives?" I asked in my nicest voice. "This is very important."

I'm not sure what that tattooed man deemed important— or if he was going to demand details. I wasn't about to admit to him that my new love was a werewolf.

He obviously didn't think I was the type to be hanging around a tattoo parlor and didn't seem to want to be further bothered by my presence. I waited outside his shop as he popped inside—afraid the tattoo artist was going to ink Dr. Meadows's address on my back. Instead, he returned quietly and was kind enough to write it down on a piece of paper.

I followed his directions closely.

I arrived at a two-story cottage home that appeared delightfully magical. Wood-carved sculptures lined the yard. Orbs of every color dotted what must have been a summertime garden. Ceramic and mosaic tiles spelled out New Age affirmations. Artistic symbols of every religion hung from the porch. I was met with the tune of a thousand wind chimes clanging in the breeze. I knocked on her door.

Dr. Meadows answered. Her long gray hair was frizzy,

and she covered her flowing blouse with a South American shawl.

"I'm sorry to bother you, Dr. Meadows. But do you remember me?"

I could see she was trying to place me. I was all bundled up from the cold.

"Were you the one selling candles for your school band?" she asked. "I've been waiting for them to be delivered."

I lowered my hoodie. "No. I came to your store for a reading with my friends."

"Oh yes, of course."

"Please, I must talk to you. I need your help."

"I wasn't expecting company, but please, come in."

Dr. Meadows's house was not unlike her store. It felt warm and cozy, and the scent of vanilla greeted all visitors. Dreamcatchers hung against the walls, and amethysts and crystals lined every vacant space. Expensive-looking African and Native American artwork decorated her home as if it were a museum.

"You were right," I said forcefully.

"About what?"

"About everything!" I was nearly shouting.

"Calm down, let me brew you some tea."

"I don't have time for tea. Do you remember what you said to me?" I asked.

"Uh . . . I do so many readings. . . ."

"You had insight for my friends—about their personalities. But when it came to me, you said, 'Beware of the woods . . . of the sounds of howling. There could be outsiders who will turn . . . underneath the glow of the full moon.'"

"Ah, yes. I do remember."

"Why did you say what you did to me?"

"It was just a feeling."

"When I left your store, I decided to walk home. There was a blizzard. I got caught in it. And then, I was surrounded by a pack of wolves."

"You must be joking." She was as skeptical of me as I'd originally been of her.

"I'm not."

"How on earth did you survive?" she asked.

"The outsider. He saved me."

Even Dr. Meadows seemed shocked by the accuracy of her prediction.

"But why did you say what you did to me?" I pressed again.

"I just had a feeling, that's all."

"But it came true."

"Predictions are often left to the individual's interpretation."

"You have to believe me. It happened just as you said— just as you warned me."

Dr. Meadows was speechless.

"But it's true," I said.

"Are you sure? One message could be interpreted many ways."

"Not in this case. Snow is snow. Howling is howling." I tried to persuade her.

"It couldn't be," she argued.

"But it could. It did. You knew."

"I did?"

It was then we both realized the impact of our situation.

She rose, her face glowing like a crystal in the sunlight. "All these years . . ." she muttered to herself.

I couldn't believe it. I was having to convince Dr. Meadows that she was psychic.

"No one has believed you?" I asked.

"But you have free will," she said in a daze.

"Yes, I do. But you predicted it. And I should have listened."

She sat down as if her energy had been spirited away.

"It's true, Dr. Meadows. Everything you told me came true. And now you have to help me."

"Help you?" she asked, confused. "But you made it safely out of the woods."

"Well . . . It's not me who needs help, really. But before I tell you . . . is there some sort of psychic-client privilege—like an attorney-client one?"

"I don't think so . . ."

"I mean this must be a secret."

"Maybe you should tell a priest. Or a rabbi. Or a school counselor." She was shying away from taking any further responsibility in the matter.

"No—I have to tell you. No one else will understand."

Dr. Meadows was hesitant. "All right. Go ahead."

"You said beware of a kiss underneath a full moon."

"Yes?"

"I kissed a guy. And he changed . . ."

"Go on."

"Into a . . ."

"An animal?" she asked.

"Well, sort of."

"Honey, they all do." She laughed. "That's all you wanted to tell me?"

"Dr. Meadows, you have to believe me. There is a guy in this town, and when there is a full moon, he turns . . ."

"Turns into what?"

"A werewolf."

"A werewolf?" Dr. Meadows was incredulous. This time she let out a laugh that shook the candles flickering on her coffee table. "Honey, now I think this may be something for the school nurse. . . ."

"Dr. Meadows—you have all those books in your store about witches and warlocks. I thought you believed it all."

"I do believe in some—I've based my life's work on the supernatural. I've seen and felt apparitions and other paranormal events. But I'm sure that I'm not the first person in the world who doesn't believe in werewolves."

"But you must. You are the only person I know who can help him," I urged. "Dr. Meadows—" I pleaded. But the psychic remained silent.

"I only know what I told you."

"You know things that others don't. You need to help my friend. Before it's too late. The moon will be full again soon."

Now Dr. Meadows grew concerned. "This isn't something I can change with a moment's notice. I have to consult books and spells. And . . ."

I saw dollar signs in her eyes. "I just have a small allowance. But I'll give you all of it—"

She studied me, as if now realizing that I might be telling her the truth.

"This must remain a secret," I said. "You are the only person I've told. Not even my best friends or my parents know what happened."

"I will need to observe him. Both when the moon is waxing and of course when it is full."

"I don't think that is possible now. He's forbidden me to see him."

"He is angry?" she asked. "He blames you? Us?" She was suddenly afraid. "You haven't told him where I live, have you?"

"Of course not. And besides, he's not mad or vengeful. That's the point. This guy is different from anyone I've ever met before. He refuses to be near me at night because he's afraid he's dangerous."

"Well, if what you say is true and he is a werewolf, you must stay away from him. For your own safety."

"So, you believe me?" I asked.

"Yes, I do," she said. "But I must see him. As soon as possible."

I gave Dr. Meadows a huge hug. Her warm personality crept through her embrace. Finally, part of my guilt was assuaged. "Thank you. I feel better already."

As she opened the door for me, the wind outside was still. Dr. Meadows grasped my shoulder as if something overcame her. "You must never kiss a werewolf," she warned vehemently.

She shut the door behind me, and the chimes rang out wildly. Suddenly I didn't feel so at ease anymore.

I wasn't sure how I'd convince Brandon to let Dr. Meadows meet him with the full moon approaching. He wasn't keen on me being with him under these circumstances, and she wasn't the kind of doctor who was certified by the medical board. How was I going to let a perfect stranger hang out in the woods and watch him transform into a lycan? There was so much Brandon was dealing with at once—but perhaps he'd be comforted by someone trying to help him. I decided to text him with my news. As I waited for his response, I continued research on my essay. However, I didn't find any information on the effects of kissing a werewolf. I was so attracted to Brandon—by day and by night—all I could do was imagine kissing him. If I was warned not to, I wasn't sure what the implications might be. Maybe I'd turn into a werewolf, or maybe it would be his demise. It wasn't fair that I wasn't supposed to kiss the one guy I was desperate to be with. Instead, I clung to his shirt as if it were him.

And not knowing why—or what might happen—if I kissed a werewolf only made the torment worse. And if I was in agony, I could only imagine the torment Brandon faced alone at school or by night in the woods.

I was alone, too. I'd always had Ivy to lean on and help me through situations. This time I'd have to figure out the answers on my own. My life had been easier and much less complicated before Brandon Maddox arrived at Legend's Run, but I wouldn't trade knowing him for the peace I had then.

NINETEEN

watching wolves

The following morning in English class I wasn't able to concentrate. My calendar told me all I needed to know. There was going to be a full moon tonight. I could see the pale white of the moon in the bright blue sky from my classroom window—it was just waiting to shine its glow. Mrs. Clark was reminding us to finish our folklore essays and I knew I hadn't completed mine. The only werewolf I wanted to write about was the one sitting a few rows behind me.

Mrs. Clark's attention suddenly turned outside. It appeared she, too, was having a hard time focusing on our lesson. But she looked concerned. She instructed us to remain seated and told us she'd return shortly.

I had a seat next to the window, so I glanced over to see what the object of her attention was. Fifty yards away from our classroom was the Legend's High flagpole. Standing next to it was a wolf.

It was jarring. I immediately surveyed the outlying area to see if any students were in danger. Fortunately, there weren't any students lingering anywhere.

"It's a wolf!" Ivy screamed, catching sight of it, too.

My classmates all rose and bolted for the window. They pulled out their concealed cell phones and began taking videos and pictures of the wolf.

The wolf began to howl, a strident howl. It sent shivers down my spine. The scene was surreal—a wild animal roaming around campus as if this was its home. And if that wasn't bizarre enough, out from the woods behind the gym came two more wolves and they joined the first wolf's side.

"They're taking over the school!" Ivy yelled.

Other windows around the school filled with students' quizzical faces.

For some reason, the wolves were focusing their attention toward our classroom and began walking in our direction.

"They're coming for us," one of the students said.

Nash remained seated. I could see the color drain from his face. I feared for my ex, knowing his immense aversion to canines. I didn't feel anger toward him but rather protection. Our windows were at least twenty feet off the ground and we were in no impending danger.

"There's no way they can come in here," I said, hoping to comfort Nash. "Unless they have a ladder."

We were all glued to the view of several wolves looking up at us as if they were about to join our lesson. Cameras flashed, a few students screamed, while other classmates were calling or texting.

The scene was truly frightening. Even though I assured myself that we had a brick-and-concrete wall between us and a few feet in height, the sight of wild animals focusing their attention on us was terrifying. Ivy clung to me. Most of the guys thought it was really cool and whooped and howled. A few jocks waved and taunted the wolves.

"You mustn't do that," Ivy warned. "You'll only provoke them."

"I'd love to pet one," Abby said. "They look so beautiful."

"They are wolves!" Ivy said. "They aren't pets."

The school administrator's voice came over the loudspeaker.

"Everyone please remain in your seats and in your classrooms with your doors and windows locked. We are under a Code Yellow. I repeat. Code Yellow. No one is to leave the classrooms or building at this time. We will inform you when it is safe to resume the normally scheduled day."

Now I was frightened.

Just then Mrs. Clark returned to our classroom and instructed us to immediately take our seats. She secured the door and double-checked to make sure all the windows were locked. A pack of wolves was such an unusual sight, even she hung by the window as we all peered from our seats.

Within a few minutes, there were at least five wolves howling outside our window.

I glanced back at Brandon—the only other student who had remained seated through all of the chaos. He had his head buried in his textbook. I wondered what was going through his lycan mind.

I couldn't imagine why the wolves were here—if it was purely coincidence, if they were lost, or if there was some paranormal connection. Mrs. Clark tried to resume her lecture, but it was impossible with five howling wolves focusing on our classroom.

"This is so freaky!" Ivy said.

"They are cool," Abby said.

"They could rip your head off," Dylan said.

"They must be following you," Ivy teased me. "Everywhere you go there are wolves!"

"I wonder if we'll be on the news," Abby said excitedly.

I was still scared. I clung onto my writing binder as if it could protect me. The situation was so unreal. And although I knew we were safely locked inside, the threat of a pack of wolves outside our window was disturbing.

Finally, a few police cars pulled into our school's entrance. An animal control car followed closely behind.

"We can calm down now," Mrs. Clark said. "Animal control is here."

We eyed the outside action, some of the students sitting

on top of their desks for a better view.

Several officers stepped out of their cars covered in protective gear and using their open doors for further protection. A few animal control wardens came out of their cars with tranquilizer guns and nets.

"They're going to shoot them," I said.

"They have to," Ivy said. "Did you think the police were going to handcuff the wolves and put them in the back of a squad car?"

"Let's return to our lesson," Mrs. Clark said, her voice unsteady. But no one focused on our teacher.

"Brandon," Mrs. Clark said. "Please remain in your seat."

I could feel the presence of someone walking by me.

Brandon brushed past me and headed to the window.

"Brandon," Mrs. Clark said. "Get away from the window! You must sit down!"

But Brandon ignored her. Instead he took off a glove and placed the palm of his wounded hand on the pane of glass. He stared down at the leader of the pack, transfixed.

The wolves stopped howling. Brandon and the wolves locked gazes, as if the wolves were hypnotized by Brandon's stare.

It was spellbinding to watch. I didn't know what was happening, but the tiny hairs on my skin and the back of my neck tingled.

"What is he doing?" Ivy asked.

Brandon continued to stare at the leader of the pack.

"He thinks he's talking to the wolves," Abby said.

The wolves remained fixated on Brandon as if he was their trainer, as if Brandon was one of them and they were looking up to him as their new leader.

The police held their stance by their patrol cars, apparently working out their plan of action. The animal controllers, now at least twenty yards away, slowly crept toward the wolves.

Just then the leader of the wolves howled at Brandon.

As the handlers took aim, the pack tore off. They raced away from the campus and disappeared into the woods behind the gym.

Mrs. Clark, my classmates, and I watched in astonishment as Brandon replaced his glove and calmly walked back to his desk and took his seat.

I was dumbfounded. Along with my classmates, we were perplexed, confused, and amazed at what we'd just witnessed. It was as if we all were wondering if we had really just seen a student, one who didn't speak in class or make himself known, communicating with a pack of wolves. We looked to Brandon for answers, but by the way he was avoiding all eye contact or questions, it was clear he wasn't about to give any.

"That was totally freaky!" Ivy said. "Did you see what I just saw?"

"Yes! I swear they were looking right at Brandon," Abby confirmed. "I think he was talking to them."

The classroom was abuzz with gossiping, laughter, and disorder. The students glared at Brandon, bewildered. Mrs. Clark tapped her desk with her pointer.

I gazed back at Brandon. His face was flushed from all the attention, and he was doing his best to hide behind his textbook.

"They must have sensed the police coming," I said out loud. "Wolves are very intuitive that way."

Legend's Run High was buzzing with the wolf sightings. The lunchroom was packed with students replaying videos, showing pictures, and telling their version of the events that had occurred by the flagpole.

Ivy insisted Brandon had something to do with the wolves retreating, but everyone in our group laughed at her hypothesis.

"I was sitting right there!" she said.

"So was I," I said. "They left as soon as the animal controllers started to approach them."

"He took off his glove—the one he always wears," she said. "Don't you think that was freaky?"

"Maybe he was nervous and got warm," I said. "We all were excited."

"He was talking to them," she said. "Like the Wolfman."

They all laughed again, but I remained silent.

"You have to admit, it was pretty freaky," Jake agreed.

"Maybe it was coincidence, but why did he go up there in the first place?"

"He might have psychic powers," Abby teased. "Like Dr. Meadows. Maybe he can give us our next reading."

"We always thought he was strange," Ivy said. "Ever since he arrived here at school." She looked to Abby for help.

My friends agreed.

"But that doesn't mean he can talk to wolves," I said.

"Why do you always defend him?" Ivy asked.

"Yes, why?" Nash suddenly chimed in.

Everyone waited for my response.

"Because no one else will," I finally said.

When I turned on my phone during lunch, there were at least five voice messages and a dozen texts from my mom. I immediately called to assure her I was safe and the school and community resources had done their best to protect us and maintain order.

"It's all over the news," she said when I arrived home. My mom left work early and had been watching the TV all day. "They closed several businesses around the school. I'm so glad you're home safe."

We were glued to the local four o'clock news. Animal experts talked about wolf safety, but most agreed that it was uncommon for one wolf to venture out of the woods in the middle of the day and come so close to an area with a human population. For a pack of wolves to do it was extraordinary.

The sun was going to be setting soon. I didn't have much sunlight left before the full moon was going to shine. I was worried about Brandon and what might happen to him.

"I have to run out—but I'll be back soon," I said, grabbing my coat.

"You're not going anywhere tonight," my mom said. "You can't go out when there are wolves running around. Give it a few days to see how it plays out."

I was always well behaved and it was very rare that I didn't follow the rules. It was as unlikely for me to get in trouble as it was to discover that a transfer student could become a werewolf. But both things were possible tonight.

"I'm sorry, Mom, but I have to go—" I said defiantly, closing the back door behind me.

TWENTY

six senses

The sun was beginning to set over the trees, and it wouldn't be long until the rise of the full moon. I hurried to Brandon's. I needed to see him face-to-face—and see which features stared back at me, those of a handsome guy or those of a wolf.

I found him in the backyard stacking wood into a pile alongside a small shed.

This time Brandon wasn't pleased by my presence.

"What are you doing here?" he asked. "I told you I couldn't see you. Especially tonight."

"I wanted to be near you, just like the wolves did when they came to see you at school," I confessed.

"You have to leave, Celeste." He backed away, but I followed.

"I'm not going," I said.

He picked up a few pieces of wood that had tumbled from the pile. "You have to—it's the only way."

"Then you will have to carry me off," I said, finally facing him. "And I'm much heavier than that pile of wood."

He returned the logs into the pile and stared off at the setting sun. "Celeste, what is happening to me?" he asked.

His pain and torment were palpable. I would have taken it all away if I could. I hugged him and he caved in on me.

"I don't know, Brandon. It seems odd, mystical, paranormal. Or maybe it's nothing at all. Maybe it's all coincidence."

"But I never felt anything like this before . . . until that day when I heard you calling in the woods. And then I was never the same."

"It was a full moon, then. I knew it was my fault."

"It's not—"

I'd experienced Brandon Maddox through my five senses. One, I first saw Brandon in class that day that he transferred. Two, I heard him speak when Ivy and Abby confronted him. Three, we touched that day he saved me in the woods. Four, his scent still lingered on his shirt that I kept on my nightstand. Five, I had tasted his lips against mine. But there was one more sense I was desperate to witness; I needed to confirm my suspicions through the sixth sense—the paranormal.

"I'm not leaving," I said.

"You have to go—I don't know how I'll be—or what I'll be."

I held on to him with all my strength. "It's okay."

I wanted to see for sure if what we'd experienced under the last full moon was coincidence or could be explained away by another reason—one other than legends, folklore, or predictions.

The full moon shone down upon us as Brandon enveloped me in his arms and kissed me. He was so passionate and intense, I was afraid I was going to be the one who would have to throw off my coat this time.

Brandon was kissing my neck when he suddenly broke away.

"What is it?" I asked.

"I'm burning up. Like the sun is lighting me on fire—only there's no sun."

"Just the moon . . ." I barely managed to say.

"You must leave. Now!"

I had Brandon's shirt at home, so I knew last month's episode wasn't a dream. But that didn't mean I'd seen what I thought I'd seen. Tonight, I wouldn't let Brandon out of my sight. I had to see the transformation for myself.

Brandon's blue eyes turned intensely gray. He covered them and retreated. He went into the woods, using trees to block my view. He was desperate for me not to see him, but I followed him anyway. I ran past trees and jumped over fallen branches and trudged through snow. By the time I caught up to him, his hair was savagely long and lush. His face sported that sexy goatee I'd seen before, and his well-muscled arms and chest were covered with a thin layer of hair. He let out a howl.

Like last time, I backed away. My instincts told me to run for my life.

But there was something drawing me to Brandon, to this strange and powerful figure, something more than just his magnetic muscles and chiseled abs. It was his soul.

Even so, I was scared. For him and for me.

He breathed heavily. His chest heaved; his ribs were like those of a lean animal. His stare was hypnotic; I could barely stand in his presence. I wondered if, like Juliette said, he'd carry me off into the woods. Part of me wanted to escape; the other yearned to find out what might happen if I stayed—if I could help him, since this was all my fault.

I debated running, attempting to leave the uncertainty of woods on the hilltop for the safety of my home—a simple place where werewolves were on TV or were the subjects of students' essays. However, I knew it would be impossible to outrun Brandon. In this lycan form he was powerful, perhaps invincible, and, to me, deadly attractive and soulful.

But Brandon appeared frightened about what he was capable of doing. He began to retreat. I sensed his turmoil. I wanted to stay, but he wanted me to go.

I shook my head and didn't move. If he had wanted to kill me, he would have tried to already. I was safe with him for now. I extended my hand to him. I tried my best to remain calm, but my shaking revealed my fear.

Brandon's brow furrowed and his piercing fangs were shining. His gray gaze bore through me.

I took a deep breath and focused on my task.

"It's okay," I said, my voice quavering. "I want to help you."

"You can't be near me like this." His voice was low and seductive.

Brandon was more alone than I'd ever seen him before—more alone than he'd been as a new student walking the halls of a cliquey school, more than a misunderstood outsider quietly eating his lunch in solitude, more than a guy living in a small guesthouse behind his grandparents' home, with his father a continent away.

I inched forward. Brandon didn't attack me. He didn't run away, either.

I took his hand, which was sporting masculine brown hair.

When we touched it was as if I could know his soul. Feelings of love, fear, loneliness, and euphoria raced through me as if we were one. I stared up at him. I was attracted to his spirit as much as to his shirtless body. By touching him, everything I thought I sensed about his feelings from across the hallway, lunchroom, or class I now felt as well, magnified a thousand times.

Then my fingers grazed his palm and the raised scar from his wolf bite. It was bright red, as if the moonlight had branded its radiance into his skin.

I placed his hand to my heart. I wanted to let him know I was here for him, like he'd been there for me.

"A wolf bit you under a full moon," I said. "I guess the Legend's Run Werewolf folklore is true. If you hadn't saved me, then this wouldn't have happened to you. And then the kiss—it was under a full moon as well. Dr. Meadows warned me . . ." I was filled with remorse and guilt at being the one who had caused his condition. If I had heeded Dr. Meadows's warning, Brandon would have been like any other student going to school. Instead, he was a werewolf. A tear leaked and drizzled down my cheek.

"There has to be more to . . . whatever this is," he reassured me. "It's not your fault."

I adored Brandon's strength, not only physical but moral.

I reached for his face. Gingerly, I touched his goatee and stubble. He melted into my tender caress as if he'd been yearning for this touch for a lifetime.

He smelled delightfully woodsy, like burning leaves mixed with frosting snow.

He grazed the tips of his fangs along the tips of my fingers. Chills danced from them straight to my pounding heart. I felt completely spellbound, as though by being together— whether in this form or his daylight one—I felt complete. Brandon wasn't alone, and neither was I.

"Please don't go," I said. "Not yet."

There was one more thing I longed for. I felt a pull to

Brandon more than ever before. If only I could get close enough to him to feel his lips against mine. By day Brandon was handsome, and by moonlight he was stunningly gorgeous and irresistible. Whatever coursed through his veins to make him a werewolf also made him unbelievably magnetic.

Brandon perked up as if he had heard something in the distance. Then I, too, heard the cry of a wolf.

Brandon lurched away. He shook his head, his long hair flowing wildly, and held me at bay. I wasn't ready for our time together to end.

Before I knew it, I was standing in the woods alone.

His woodsy scent still lingered in the air, and my skin still danced from his touch.

But I knew now that it was true. I'd fallen in love with a werewolf.

TWENTY-ONE

into the woods

The following day, I gazed at the empty chair in the back of the classroom.

Now that I was certain Brandon was a werewolf, I knew what I'd be dealing with when the full moon showed its haunting glow. As the moon would appear full for two more evenings, he'd be absent from school for several days, likely spending his nights in the woods. All day long police and animal control cars patrolled the suburbs and school in case the wolves showed up again. The people of Legend's Run were up in arms about the strange animal behavior.

I was desperate to be with Brandon, but Ivy and Abby had wrangled me into watching Abby's volleyball game after school.

Abby's game was delayed and didn't end until just after

dusk. Ivy and Abby were going to join the other girls for a celebratory dinner, but I planned to head to Brandon's. As I left the gymnasium, I heard faint howling coming from a tree-filled lot near the back of the school. I ignored it and continued on to my car until I saw Brandon's Jeep parked by the school fence.

Two patrol cars were stationed in the middle of the student lot.

"Brandon?" I called.

I snuck into the edge of the woods without venturing in too far. I'd learned my lesson when I'd gotten lost in the blizzard. I wasn't about to put my life or anyone else's in danger.

Lights from the parking lot and gymnasium streamed in through the trees, illuminating a small portion of the woods. A fingerless-gloved hand reached out from the darkness. Brandon, in werewolf form, was leaning against a tree, smiling at me.

Happily, I took his hand and he drew me into him. He grazed his fangs against me. I touched his stubbly face. I ran my fingers through his locks, as he did the same to mine.

"I missed you today," I said.

"I hunger for you all day and night," he said as he kissed the nape of my neck.

He gazed at me. His lips were only inches from my own. I was longing inside to finally have them touch in the moonlight. *You must never kiss a werewolf.* I heard Dr. Meadows's warning in my head, but I wasn't sure if I could wait any longer.

He pulled my hair off my neck and leaned in. He breathed in as if he was inhaling me. I had dotted myself with perfume and sugary vanilla body lotion. The scent of my hair and body seemed to be intoxicating to Brandon. He tugged at my henley with his fangs and nibbled my shoulder. I was so entranced, enamored by his seductive power. I was only moments from kissing the most romantic werewolf in the world. I remembered Dr. Meadows's words but I didn't want to heed her warning. But my skepticism toward Dr. Meadows was what got Brandon into this state in the first place. What was I supposed to do?

"I don't think I should—" I said, breathless.

"I understand." Brandon must have sensed my distress.

"But that doesn't mean I don't want to—" I vowed.

He pulled away.

"I know someone who can help you—or at least wants to try," I said.

"Who?" he asked, excited.

"Dr. Meadows. She's the one who gave me the reading and warned me about the full moon."

"Does she have experience with werewolves?" he asked.

"Almost—she's a psychic."

"I know . . . but has she dealt with werewolves before?"

"Well . . ." I said, "she's never seen one."

He couldn't hide his disappointment. Brandon turned away from me. "There isn't anyone to help me—" he said.

I felt awful.

"I don't want to be some stranger's experiment," he continued.

"I understand—"

"It's hard enough making excuses to my grandparents why they don't see me for a few nights," he said. "If word gets out in town about me, then I'll have to remain in the woods during the daylight, too. I won't be able to show myself to anyone. But I've got to find a way to stop this from happening."

"Celeste?" I heard my name called from outside the woods.

"I have to go," I whispered, but Brandon had already retreated into the darkness. I heard his heavy breathing but couldn't see him to even hug him good-bye.

"Celeste! Where are you?" a girl's voice called.

I jumped out of the woods to Ivy and Abby's shock and horror.

"What are you doing in there?" Ivy asked. "Are you okay?"

"Of course I am," I said. My hair was damp from the snow and my coat soiled from brushing against the tree bark.

"What were you doing in there?" Ivy asked. "We saw your car and freaked!"

"I thought I saw someone," I said.

"Someone in the woods?" Abby said.

"There could have been wolves in there!" Ivy warned.

"Or worse!" Abby said. "Are you crazy?"

I think I was. Crazy in love, that is. But I wasn't about to tell them that.

"You've been acting so strangely lately," Ivy said, "ever since you and Nash broke up. You're hard to get hold of and always seem distracted. But we'll fix that, won't we?"

Ivy took one arm and Abby linked the other. Both girls escorted me back to my car and followed me as I drove out of the school parking lot.

I was lucky I had friends who watched out for me. It was one of the many reasons I didn't want anything to jeopardize my relationship with them.

The following day I stopped in Penny for Your Thoughts again. It was the third glowing of the full moon and I wanted to see if I could finally get help for Brandon.

I waited for a client to leave and another one to pay for some amethyst geode bookends. I was getting so agitated I was almost pleading for her herbal tea.

"He doesn't want anyone to see him," I told Dr. Meadows when the store was finally empty of customers. "Can you still help him?"

"I'm afraid not," she said.

"Please," I begged. "Don't you have a crystal charm or some of those teas you make? Surely you have something I can just give to him."

"I need to see him to properly diagnose him," she said emphatically.

"You have to believe me. When it's a full moon he turns into a werewolf. I didn't believe it myself at first, but there really isn't any other explanation."

"A doctor can't give a prescription to someone they've never met."

However, the patient had to be willing to be seen. And in this case, I'd have to do more convincing.

"Then I must see him, tonight," Dr Meadows pressed. "Tell me where he will be."

"I don't know," I said. "The woods."

"Which ones?"

I shrugged.

"Then bring him to me before sunset," she said. "I'll meet you here at my shop. Then I can help him."

Dr. Meadows was pushing me in one direction while Brandon was pushing me in another. With all my research for my own essay and helping Brandon, the only cure I'd found was a silver bullet. And that definitely wasn't an option.

I knew Brandon didn't want anyone to see him after the sun set. I would do my best to delicately broach the subject again with him, but if I pushed him too hard, he wouldn't want to be around me, either.

TWENTY-TWO

a date with a werewolf

On Saturday morning, I woke up without knowing what to do next. Ivy and Abby had insisted I join them and Nash at the mall. I couldn't convince Ivy that today wasn't good. Once she got something in her head, there was no changing her mind. There wasn't much daylight in the winter months and I didn't have much time, so I'd have to make my visit with them quick in order to still have time to convince Brandon to go with me to Penny for Your Thoughts before the sun set.

I wanted to take a quick stroll with Champ prior to heading out. It would give me a chance to get some fresh air and maybe some fresh ideas on how to convince Brandon to meet Dr. Meadows. As soon as we hit the end of our street, Champ was barking wildly. I did my best to calm him down, but all the dogs in the neighborhood were barking as we passed by their houses. Champ was growling toward the wooded area behind the snow-filled soccer field, and I began to wonder if I should be worried about wolves, even with Champ along with me. I started pulling him back toward home when "Fly Me to the Moon" started playing from my back pocket. I was exhilarated. It was Brandon.

"I'm right behind you," he said when I answered the phone breathlessly.

I spun around. There was a figure standing next to the woods beyond the soccer field; it was the exact direction in which Champ was barking.

I tried my best to hold on to Champ's leash but he broke loose. I chased after him down the hill.

As soon as Champ reached Brandon, my out-of-control dog was suddenly silent.

Without so much as a command or a treat, Champ sat down and faced Brandon.

"You have a way with animals," I said when I finally caught up.

"And girls, I hope."

I wanted to kiss Brandon so badly my heart hurt.

Brandon petted Champ as if he were his own dog.

"I'd like to take you out on a real date," Brandon said. "But I know there are many complications with that. I mean, there's Nash, for one, and me being from the wrong side of town . . . and of course we'd have to be back before sunset."

"But I'm not dating Nash," I tried to assure him. "And to me, any side of town you live on is the right side."

He smiled a sweet smile.

"I should have listened to Dr. Meadows," I said.

"I don't know why you blame yourself."

"If I hadn't been so skeptical of her prediction, none of this would have happened."

"Celeste—there is no way you could have known. Besides, it's not like Dr. Meadows predicted the future. She said things that anyone could have said to you."

"I know—but it happened. Perhaps she really knew."

"And what if she didn't? What if it was just coincidence? Or you read too much into her reading?"

"But she's the only one I know who can help you," I said wearily. "She wants to see you. She says that is the only way she can help you. And if you don't go, then you might be a werewolf . . . forever." Tears began to well in my eyes.

"It's okay . . ." he said, putting his arm around me.

I couldn't even bear to look at him.

"I'll meet her," he said.

"You will?"

"Yes, if it will make you happy."

I gave him a huge hug. I didn't care whether the neighbors saw me do it, even though I knew we were hidden away.

"I'll just take Champ home and I can drive us."

"We're going now?" he asked.

"What's wrong?"

"I was hoping I'd get to see you today—for a real date. But it seems like you already have plans."

"I do—but I can see you later tonight." I realized I might have been too eager.

"Because it occurred to me," he continued, "since I can't remember the nights, I don't know how I am when the moon shows . . . I don't want you to be in any danger, so I thought I'd just try to get a glimpse of you before sunset."

"You haven't hurt me before when you've been in your werewolf form," I said. "And I've seen you change twice. What makes you think you would harm me now?"

He turned away. "I don't know what I'm like, Celeste."

I would love a real date with Brandon, but convincing him to be with me while in his werewolf form was another thing.

"Then let me be with you and I'll tell you tomorrow what you were like. I'll be able to reassure you."

I wanted to see him again as a werewolf, with his magnetic features. And since he needed to know what he was like in his werewolf form, I could tell him. I'd been waiting for months to have a real date with Brandon. Dr. Meadows had only been waiting for a few hours.

I could see that Brandon was torn.

"I'll bring Champ," I said. "If that will make you feel better. He can protect me."

"Against a werewolf?" he asked.

"I don't think either one of us is in any danger. I know

you don't remember, but I do. You could have hurt me last time—I fell and you could have overpowered me, but you didn't. Instead it looked like you were going to help me."

"Okay, then," he relented. "Will you meet me tonight?" he asked. "In the woods behind my house?"

I nodded excitedly. It was official: our first real date.

"You won't remember," I said. "But I'll be there."

"I'll remember this," he said, and pulled me into an embrace and kissed me.

As soon as he left, Champ began barking again in the direction Brandon had gone.

When I arrived at Brandon's hilltop hideout in the woods behind his grandparents' house, the scene was magical. Tiny snowflakes danced down from the sky.

Brandon was waiting for me next to a bonfire. He was as majestic and handsome as I'd ever seen him. The fire crackled and lit his features. His dark hair was tousled and sexy. I walked up to him, and I could feel the heat radiating off his body as strongly as from the campfire. I was addicted to Brandon Maddox. He wasn't like anyone I'd ever met. During the day, I found him to be a sensitive, caring guy—unlike all the guys I'd ever hung out with—and when the sun set and the full moon glowed, he was wild and irresistible. He had fangs that could pierce a girl's soul.

Champ was silent at my side. It was as if he was as mesmerized by Brandon as I was.

All at once the woods filled with the sounds of howling. Champ began to bark, too.

It was then I noticed the eyes of several wolves peeking from the dark edges of the clearing. Champ was still. Normally he would have lurched forward and I'd have been thrown into the snow. Instead, all the animals were tranquil.

I was frozen with fear. Too recently, wolves had surrounded me and I feared for my life.

"Don't be afraid," Brandon assured me. "It's okay."

I stood behind him, and Champ did, too.

The wolves, one by one, lay down in the pure white snow. The sight of the gorgeous gray wolves, which looked soft and sweet instead of fierce and dangerous, was unbelievably breathtaking. It was as magical as any footage I'd seen on animal and nature programs—only this was real.

Brandon happily petted the wolves, which were as playful as any domestic dog.

"Don't try this at home," he teased. "But do you want to try it with me?"

"I'm not sure." The wolves were amazingly beautiful. A smaller one came forward. Brandon nodded to me, and under his careful watch I suddenly felt safe. I reached out and gently touched the wolf pup. Its fur was soft and luxurious; I caressed the adorable wolf just as I had petted Champ for so many years.

It nuzzled up to me and licked my cheeks, causing me to burst out giggling.

"Okay now—" Brandon said to the pup. "Now you are getting on my territory."

He whistled, and the wolf retreated from me and returned to the pack. They all hunkered around Brandon.

Brandon seemed more at peace than I'd seen him since his arrival in Legend's Run. These wolves comforted him— like Champ comforted me.

Brandon took me in his arms. Normally, in a situation such as this one, I'd be terrified. I was in the woods, surrounded by wolves, and in the company of a werewolf. But with Brandon, I felt at ease. I must have been under his spell.

"I must say, I've never had a date like this one," I said.

"Me neither," he said.

"But if you don't remember," I said, "you could be bringing cheerleaders back here every night."

"I promise you that isn't happening."

I gave him a kiss on his cheek.

"I'm starved," he said.

He pointed to the fire, where several steaks were cooking. I peered over them.

"Where did you get these?" I asked.

"I don't remember . . ." he said.

My stomach turned. It couldn't be. A once-cute deer with Bambi's face now lying on this fire? I turned away.

"I'm only kidding," he said. "They're from my grandmother's freezer."

I sighed with relief. Brandon was such an animal lover

he'd be even more devastated than me if he discovered he'd been hunting wildlife.

We sat down together on a huge fallen tree.

He tugged at the steaks with a stick as they sizzled.

I looked around for a backpack or a picnic basket. "Any plates? Forks?"

"Oh no—I forgot," he said. "What was I thinking?"

Brandon speared one of the steaks with a small branch and handed it to me.

"I guess I'm not a gentleman after all," he said, embarrassed, as I eyed the skewered meat.

"I prefer you in the wild," I said.

He tore into his steak as if he hadn't eaten in weeks. I wasn't used to camping—my experience with campfire dining was just bringing snacks from home like our sixsome had done this past fall.

I held the branch, the meat hanging on it. This was a lot different from roasting marshmallows. If Ivy could see me now, she'd faint. Not only would I have to eat with my fingers, an activity that Ivy found revolting, but I didn't even have a napkin. I had mild trepidation, feeling like an animal myself. But I didn't want to offend Brandon, and I wasn't about to spoil our first date together.

"I'm sorry," he said. "We're really roughing it."

Though I felt uncomfortable eating in an unladylike way on a first date, there was a part of me that felt free. All these years I'd played by the rules, and it was slightly liberating to eat in the wild.

"I'll have to stop at a camping supply place after school."

"I'll remind you," I said.

If Brandon didn't remember this night together, maybe this was my chance to say things to him I wouldn't be able to say during the day. I could use this opportunity and finally confess my love to him. And in the morning, when I brushed past him at school, he wouldn't be aware that I'd already bared the depths of my soul. However, Brandon did say he recalled certain images when he awoke. And with my luck, the one where I confessed my love and he laughed in my face would be that moment. So I nibbled on my steak as daintily as I could.

Brandon devoured his steak and threw the bone to his wolf pack. He took mine when I was done, then washed his hands off in a clump of snow. Brandon put his arms around me. He gave off as much heat as the crackling fire.

"This is the best date I've ever had," I said truthfully.

The night was enchanting. The snow had stopped falling, and now the clouds parted and the icicles glistened in the moonlight. Brandon warmed my hands in his. We watched as the wolves playfully bit each other and rolled around together in the snow. Then they yawned and stretched, and before I knew it, the wolves, along with Champ, were lying sound asleep. The trees were lined with snow, and I was in the company of a magnificent wild animal of the lycan kind.

The full moon shone above us. Brandon leaned into me and rested his stubbled cheek against mine. I wanted so badly to kiss him, but I recalled Dr. Meadows's words. I couldn't take the chance. For both our sakes I had to pull away.

"I'm not supposed to kiss you when you're like this," I told him.

"Then what if I kiss you?"

He drew me back and kissed my neck, then nibbled his way to my shoulders. He nuzzled his nose along my neckline. He touched my hair and breathed it in as if the scent placed him under a spell.

I spent the rest of the evening trying to avoid kissing a werewolf.

TWENTY-THREE

mr. worthington

As I reached the reception desk of Pine Tree Village, Mr. Worthington caught sight of me. He was standing in the lobby next to a grand piano.

"Celeste. It always warms my heart to see you," he said, his fingers tinkling on the keys. "What is new with you?"

"You wouldn't believe it if I told you," I said seriously.

"I've heard a lot in my time, young lady. Nothing would surprise me."

I knew if I told Mr. Worthington my recent events, he might have a coronary right there and then. I couldn't be responsible.

"Are you referring to the wolves showing up at your school?" he asked.

"Did you hear about them?" I'd almost forgotten.

"It's all anyone is talking about. Please. I'd love to hear an eyewitness account."

"It was so strange. They were outside my classroom. Beautiful, with fluffy gray-and-white fur. If they weren't so dangerous, I would have taken one home with me."

"Well, their bite is much worse than their bark," he said.

I cracked a smile.

"It is odd for wolves to come so close to the human population," he said.

"That's what I've heard."

"It must have been because of the full moon," he said mysteriously.

Just then a nurse came up to him. "It's time for your meds," she said.

I followed Mr. Worthington back to his room. He had tons of pictures and mementos hung on the walls and placed around tables and shelves to remind him of his accomplishments and family.

He took the colorful pills the nurse handed him, and she left us to continue our conversation.

"So are you back to hear more about the Legend's Run Werewolf?" he asked.

"Yes," I said. "Last time I came you said you were only at the beginning of your story."

"Come, sit down," he said, pointing to an antique chair.

"This is my great-grandfather," he added, showing me a worn black-and-white portrait of a man. "Some say he was mentally ill. Others say he was cursed. His wife swore otherwise."

I was surprised at Mr. Worthington's candor and was enraptured by his biography.

"My great-grandfather was building his house—it was over in the western part of town by the river—when a pack of wolves came after his baby, sleeping in a bassinet by the lumber pile. That baby was my father."

I was riveted by his story and I nodded, hoping he'd continue.

"By the time he caught sight of the pack, one wolf already had the basket in its mouth, ready to carry it back to its den.

"As his wife cried out, he fought like mad, desperate to save his son. The boy, still cradled in the basket, was unharmed, but my great-grandfather was almost killed. Bloody and on the brink of death, he lay under a shade tree as his wife ran for help. The local chieftain came to his aid and attended to him. When the chieftain finally left, he told my family my great-grandfather would live but the wolf was now inside him—in his blood.

"But no one knew what the chieftain meant at the time. Apparently my great-grandfather was never the same."

It was just like Brandon. Suddenly I was dying to tell Mr. Worthington my tale of the Legend's Run Werewolf. But he wasn't finished with his story, and I wasn't sure it was wise to tell Brandon's secret.

"It started with a full moon and continued for three days.

He roamed the woods alone. When he was spotted by hunters he was mistaken for a wolf."

Mr. Worthington showed me more pictures. Many were black-and-white photos. Others were in color but worn. Then he showed me an old family portrait. "This is his wife and my father," he said. Then he handed me a black-and-white baby picture. "And this is yours truly."

"Ah . . . You were so cute!" I said.

"And this is my wife, my son, Harry, and his daughter, Claire," he said, pointing to still more photos. "She's something of a wild child. Always was. Couldn't be kept down by conventional traditions. She married a man, here in Legend's Run, and had a child. As soon as the child was born, she disappeared. She ran off to a commune and we lost contact with her many years ago. I always told my wife it was the wolf in her blood."

"Your great-grandfather was the Legend's Run Werewolf," I said. "Now, that is a great story!"

I couldn't shake from my mind the tale Mr. Worthington had shared with me. It might have been because he'd had too much time on his hands or he, like in the traditions of folklore that were the subject of my essay, was passing down the town's legend. I'm sure everyone in town had a similar anecdote—people grasping onto the idea of something mysterious existing to keep the town exciting.

Just a few weeks ago it would have shocked me that

someone as wise and rational as Mr. Worthington would latch on to something so extraordinary and believe it was true. It wasn't the kind of story in which you say that your family's ancestors are royalty. Mr. Worthington wasn't trying to convince me that he was kin to a king but rather that he was related to a werewolf.

I wouldn't have believed it for a minute if I hadn't fallen in love with a werewolf myself.

I returned home and wolfed down my lunch. It was always good to get some home time on a weekend, but I was bursting to tell Brandon about my encounter with Mr. Worthington. He might laugh it off or find comfort knowing someone I knew insisted that they, too, believed in werewolves. When I headed out the back door, I found someone waiting for me in the driveway. It was Nash.

This was the first time we'd been alone in weeks.

"You canceled the other night," Nash said. "We all were going to the mall. I had to watch Abby and Ivy shop for two hours. What gives?"

It was clear Nash was feeling lonely.

"Where are you off to in such a hurry? Volunteering again?"

"No, I already did that."

"Then what's up?" he asked.

"Just errands."

"Why are you wearing those atrocious gloves? Seems to

me you're copying someone else's style."

"They make fingerless gloves, you know, because people wear them."

"People, yes, but you?"

"You're overthinking it," I replied defensively. But was he really? I was wearing them for the exact reason Nash thought I was—to be like Brandon. I couldn't admit it to him, or anyone else. It was best to deflect the attention I was bringing to myself and Brandon.

"So, is it love?" Nash asked.

"What do you mean?" I was startled by his directness.

"Are you in love?"

"What are you talking about? In love with whom?"

He took my hand.

"I'd like us to get back together." He took my other hand and pulled me close. "You want me to pay attention to you. I get that. So I will."

I liked Nash. He was handsome and popular and had moments of being a great boyfriend. Before we'd begun dating, I'd had a crush on him since I could remember. Every girl did. But as gorgeous and athletic as he was, we ultimately had different values and goals. And I was in love with another guy.

"I don't think we should keep seeing each other," I said. "We want different things."

Nash dropped my hands in disgust. He paused, his face flushed red.

"You'll see," he said. "You'll be begging to go back out with me. You mark my words."

My ex-boyfriend hopped in his car and sped off into the distance.

I still wanted to tell Brandon about Mr. Worthington's remarks. The only thing on my mind was being in his arms. But I arrived at his house to find him holding something else—groceries.

He was helping a woman get produce out of her hatchback.

Brandon hurried over to me carrying several bags.

"Hey, Celeste," he said.

"Hi. Did I come over at a bad time?"

"No, I'm just helping out. I'd like you to meet someone."

I followed Brandon to the car. A very stately woman with perfectly styled brown hair greeted me with a smile that looked remarkably like Brandon's.

"Grandma, this is Celeste."

"Hi, Celeste. It is wonderful to meet you."

"You, too, Mrs. Maddox."

"You can call me Barb," she continued sweetly. "I am so happy Brandon has a friend," she said as if she was taking me under her wing. "I worried so when he moved here after school had already begun. Well, I am so happy to know why he's been keeping to himself and acting so . . ." She rolled her eyes. "Now I know why he's been behaving so strangely," she said, winking at me. "Would you like to come in for hot chocolate and cake?"

I looked to Brandon for an answer.

"We have to study, Gram. But thanks."

"Perhaps another time," she said, walking up the back stairs.

"Yes, I'd love to," I said.

"I'll only be a minute." Brandon followed his grandmother with the groceries and met me inside his guesthouse.

"She is so cute!" I said. "I love her."

"She is sweet, but she can be a bit . . ."

"Grandmotherish?"

"Exactly."

"Is it lonely back here, with your grandparents in the main house?"

"Not now," he said, engulfing me in his strong embrace.

We settled in his guesthouse for a quiet afternoon. We talked a little about my research into werewolf folklore and how I wondered if there could possibly be a cure that wasn't a silver bullet. I mentioned meeting Dr. Meadows again, but Brandon still wasn't sure he wanted to reveal his secret. While Brandon spent some time researching werewolves on his computer, I leafed through the books he had on his shelf. I saw a vintage Hardy Boys and pulled it out. Pictures were stuffed inside. I examined the first one.

I was stunned. Staring back at me was the same picture

Mr. Worthington had in his room. I turned the picture over and inscribed in pencil was the name Claire Worthington.

I was afraid to speak.

"Who is this woman?" I asked.

Brandon turned to me. "She's my mother."

I gasped.

"What?" he asked. "It's like you've just seen a ghost."

"I just . . ." I began.

"I haven't seen her since I was a kid," he said. "I was raised by my father."

"Brandon, I've seen this picture before."

"What? You couldn't have. Where, here?"

"I know this man at the retirement community. He's so kind, and a gentleman. We spend a lot of time talking, and recently he told me the story of his great-grandfather, who was bitten by a wolf."

"That's weird."

"He said that his great-grandfather was never the same."

"Sounds familiar."

"This man I know, his name is Charles Worthington. Do you know him?"

"No."

"He has a granddaughter. Her name is Claire Worthington."

"That must be a coincidence."

"You told me your mother's family moved away."

"Yes," he said.

"Well, no one told you that one of them moved back."

Brandon was trying to process this new information.

"It's more than coincidence, Brandon. My friend Mr. Worthington is your great-grandfather!"

surprise visitor

Ivy, Abby, and Nash and I were hanging out after school in the gymnasium. Nash and Abby were waiting for their various athletic practices to begin, and I was trying to stall until I'd be in the clear to catch up with Brandon and take him to Penny for Your Thoughts. I glanced out one of the windows and spotted a woman with long gray hair and bundled up in a tan parka roaming our campus sidewalk as if she was looking for someone in particular.

I pressed my face closer to the glass and recognized it was Dr. Meadows.

"What is she doing here?" Ivy asked, also spotting the psychic.

"I don't know," I said. "I better find out."

"Why would you want to do that?"

I headed down the bleachers and raced ahead before my friends could follow me. I opened the gymnasium doors and caught up to the psychic.

"What are you doing here?" I whispered.

"You didn't show up at my store. I was concerned something happened to you," she said.

"I've been trying to convince him to see you. It's taking some time. But I think he will."

"That is great," she said. "But it has to be soon."

"We discovered it's in his blood," I said softly. "The lycan lineage goes generations back."

"Which one is he?" she asked. "No, wait—don't tell me."

Just then my friends, their beaux, and Nash opened the gymnasium doors. Dr. Meadows pointed to Nash.

I half laughed.

"I must see him at night," she said urgently, looking at Nash.

"But it's not a full moon again for weeks."

"I know, but this way I can document him before and after. I'll bring my equipment."

"Equipment?" It sounded painful and at the very least intrusive.

I was desperate to find a cure for Brandon's condition; however, at what cost I wasn't sure.

"I must have documentation," Dr. Meadows said, stumbling on her words. "It will be okay, I promise."

"What kind of documentation?" I said. "He needs to sign something?" I pried.

"Nothing invasive. Just something I can replay. To make sure what he is experiencing is real."

"I can guarantee you it's real," I said hurriedly.

My friends were staring at us. Dr. Meadows stared back as if she was examining Nash.

Then she turned her attention to me. "I need proof in order to find out how to deal with it."

I didn't want my true love to be filmed, hooked up to electrodes or possibly other torture devices.

"I was hoping for a potion," I said. "Or some charm he could wear around his neck."

"If you are hoping for a cure, this is the only way."

I left Dr. Meadows and returned to my friends.

"What is she doing here at school?" they asked.

"She was looking for a werewolf," I said truthfully. "That woman is so crazy."

Nash continued to watch Dr. Meadows until she got into her car and drove off.

When I met Brandon after school, I admitted to him that Dr. Meadows had shown up at school and that she wanted to document him. I didn't want to trick him into doing something he wasn't prepared for or willing to participate in.

"What does she want to do?" he asked, anxiously waiting by his Jeep.

"I'm not sure—she wants to see you soon. Since the full moon won't be for a few more weeks, she wants a record of you during both times. It could be as simple as asking you questions, or as much as . . ."

"As what?"

"I'm not sure. Ivy and Abby caught up to us and I didn't want them to find out what Dr. Meadows was saying."

"She might want to take pictures or film me?" he asked.

I hung my head low. "I'm not sure what her plans are. All I know is that—uh, I don't know anything." And I was as unsure as Brandon was about whether he should go and meet with her. But today I wanted him to meet Mr. Worthington. Maybe Pine Tree Village might have more answers for him.

We hopped into Brandon's Jeep and headed out his private drive and out of Riverside. We were stopped at the traffic light by the school when I noticed the car next to us was Nash's. I ducked down.

"What's wrong?" Brandon asked.

"It's Nash. He's in the car next to us. I don't want him to see me."

"I thought you weren't seeing him anymore."

"I'm not."

"Then what's the big deal?"

"I don't know."

The light changed and Nash tore off.

I sat up. Brandon pulled into the lot of a nearby park.

"What are you doing?" I asked.

"I'm going to take you back," he said, turning the steering wheel.

"I don't want to go back. I want you to meet Mr. Worthington."

"I can find him on my own," he said.

"I'm sorry. I just reacted without thinking."

But Brandon was hurt.

"I'm sorry," I said. "Everything has been happening so fast, that's all." It was so unfair. I ran the risk of losing my lifelong friends for a guy I'd only known a short time. I wasn't sure what to do. I just knew I wanted all of them in my life.

"I don't blame you, Celeste. I don't want to put you in a position you aren't ready to be in."

Brandon pushing me away only made my need to be with him even greater. Overcome with sadness, I turned away from him and stared out the window. A couple strolled hand in hand in the park. The girl snuggled up to her boyfriend as he gazed back adoringly.

"You must hate me," I said. "I invited you to a party where you didn't have a good time. You saved me from a wolf pack that left your hand maimed. I make you feel like an outsider in your own car. And the worst thing of all—because of that moonlit kiss—you've turned into a—"

Brandon took my chin and drew me to him. "It's okay, Celeste. I think you feel you have the world's problems on your shoulders."

He brushed my hair away from my face. "You don't have

to worry so much about what is right for Ivy, Nash, or me. Just what is right for you."

Brandon was the first guy I'd ever met who understood me. If I turned away from him now, I knew I'd regret it for the rest of my life.

"Please, take me with you to see Mr. Worthington."

Brandon parked the Jeep at Pine Tree Village Retirement Community.

When we entered the building we heard a commotion coming from one of the hallways and nurses were running to someone's aid.

Suddenly there was the sound of an ambulance pulling up outside. Paramedics wheeled in a gurney to the assisted living floor. I dashed down the hallway, my own heart almost stopping.

The paramedics parked the gurney next to Mr. Worthington's door.

Tears welled up in my eyes. I turned to Brandon.

The color had washed out of his face. He'd been so close to finding a relative he'd never known and an answer to his condition that perhaps no one else could reveal.

He held on to my shoulder and I melted into his chest.

Just then Mr. Worthington stepped out of his room. I almost fainted.

"You're alive!" I said.

"I hope so," he answered. "This place isn't my idea of

heaven." He told us that Mr. Lucas, his ninety-three-year-old next-door neighbor, had fallen and broken his hip.

I was surely unhappy to hear that Mr. Lucas was hurt—but grateful to know Mr. Worthington was all right. I gave the elderly man a hug so hard, I was afraid I might break him.

"I have someone I'd like you to meet," I said, and we walked into his room.

"You have a boyfriend?" he said, trying to make me blush. "I knew there was something different about you . . . I told you that before."

Now I was blushing.

"This is Brandon Maddox," I said to Mr. Worthington, pleased to introduce the two. "His mother is Claire Worthington. This is your great-grandson."

Mr. Worthington's face went white, as if he'd just seen a werewolf. I was afraid he was going to have a heart attack right there and then.

Brandon extended his wounded hand to shake. Mr. Worthington eyed the scar and gently shook Brandon's hand.

"I haven't seen you since you were a little baby," Mr. Worthington said.

"I'm so glad to meet you—I mean see you . . . again." Brandon smiled. "My father said my mother's family moved away from Legend's Run."

"We all did," said Mr. Worthington. "But I moved back a short time ago."

Mr. Worthington and Brandon sat together. I beamed with delight as my two friends began to converse. Brandon didn't look like the lonely guy in our high school lunchroom or a lone wolf in the woods anymore.

"Your mother was a gorgeous girl," Mr. Worthington began. "We were all thrilled when she got married and settled down. I only met your father a few times, but I remember him as being a brilliant man."

"Yes," Brandon said. "He's a scientist."

"After you were born, she seemed to get restless. Maybe she couldn't handle the good things in life. And then she left, and we never heard from her again. "

Brandon nodded.

"I always said it was in her blood. Something wild, not normal."

"Do you think it might be the trait of your great-grandfather?" I asked, hinting toward Brandon's nocturnal condition.

"I always blamed him for the Worthington wild streak. But we all have to take responsibility for our own actions."

"I agree with you," Brandon said.

"You didn't tell him what I told you yesterday?" Mr. Worthington asked, almost embarrassed.

"I sort of . . ."

"Well, no one believes an old man," he said.

"I do," Brandon said. "I believe you."

Mr. Worthington's face lit up. "You are the spitting image

of my son, Harry. He believed in ghost stories, too."

"Was your great-grandfather ever cured?" I asked.

"No, and that's why I was always convinced it ran in our blood."

"I appreciate your taking the time to talk to me," Brandon said politely.

"That's all I have is time. Besides, it is so nice to finally have family in Legend's Run again."

Brandon extended his hand again. Mr. Worthington took it and hugged Brandon.

"I'd like us to meet again," Brandon said.

"I'd like that, too," Mr. Worthington said. "You know where to find me. I'm here twenty-four hours a day."

werewolf spotting

The local police officers continued patrolling the streets and developments of Legend's Run, watching for appearances of wild animals. After the wolf incident at the high school, the town was still on alert. But so far there hadn't been any more wolves spotted at school.

However, there was a rumor spreading of another unusual sighting.

Abby and I were heading to the library to meet Ivy when we passed Heidi Rosen talking excitedly to her friend outside the auditorium. Abby loathed being the last person with the inside scoop. She stopped and we pretended we needed to check out the announcements on the bulletin board. Abby leaned in toward the gossiping girls.

"I swear!" Heidi said.

"Did it touch you?" her friend asked.

"No. But I thought it might."

"It?" Abby said in a hushed tone. "I wonder what it is."

"It had gray eyes," Heidi said. "And fangs."

"I think they are talking about a wolf," Abby whispered to me.

"It stood on two legs," Heidi went on.

"Maybe it's a circus wolf," I said to Abby.

"It was a werewolf, I swear!" Heidi said to her friend. "But don't tell anyone. I know people will think I'm crazy, but I had to tell you since you're my best friend."

I was stunned. Someone had spotted Brandon. But I was confused since it wasn't a full moon. Abby and I found Ivy down by her locker.

"You will never believe what I'm going to tell you," Abby declared.

"What? Heidi Rosen said she saw a werewolf?" Ivy asked nonchalantly.

"How did you know?" Abby asked.

"Jake just told me," Ivy replied.

"Who did he hear it from?" Abby questioned her.

"Nash."

"This is so bizarre," Abby said, lost in thought.

"I know. She's really lost her mind," Ivy said. "Or maybe it's that Wolfman, Brandon Maddox," she teased.

I wasn't thrilled by my friend alluding to Brandon being a werewolf. But the reality was she was right.

"Well, maybe if Heidi stayed away from Nash, then she wouldn't be seeing things," I said.

"She's been texting him," Ivy said, defending my ex, "but he refuses to see her."

"She isn't spending any time with him," Abby said. "We've made sure of that."

"Yes, he's all about you," Ivy said.

"I've told you," I assured them. "It's okay. Nash and I are over."

Ivy tried her best to hide her frustration. "If you need time to forgive him," she said, softening, "that's okay. But please, don't take too long."

By lunchtime, rumor of Heidi's werewolf spotting had made its way around the entire school. But what was worse was the other gossip I overheard later that day. I was passing the biology lab when I heard a few tech guys talking by the door.

"I was coming back from computer club when this thing jumped out from behind a tree. I tried to get it on tape, but when I downloaded it, it was so fuzzy all you could see were trees. Here—look." He showed his friend his iPhone.

"There's nothing here," he said. "Seems you need to get glasses for your glasses."

"I saw something weird last night, too," the tech guy insisted as his friends entered the classroom. "I swear on my iPod. I saw fangs."

* * *

The next few days, the werewolf-spotting stories escalated. Everyone swore they'd had an encounter with some creature of the night, and I hadn't been able to even speak about it with Brandon. I knew he must be fraught with confusion. But the person closest to him and the situation was the one he was suddenly keeping away. He hadn't returned my calls lately, and I was worried.

Nash cornered me just as I opened the main door to exit the campus after a particularly nerve-racking day at school. "Have you seen the werewolf yet?" Nash asked.

"Not unless he's standing in front of me."

"Well, I don't believe it, either. How could anyone really see a werewolf? Besides, it's not even a full moon," he said.

"I know, that's what I thought," I said.

Nash raised an eyebrow at my serious tone but then shrugged it off.

"Although, who's to say . . ." he continued. "Maybe any moon can turn them. Wolves come out every night. Why wouldn't a werewolf? Why would he wait for only a full moon to claim his next victim?"

I shuddered at his suggestion. Wasn't it enough for Brandon to change under the full moon? Now we'd have to deal with all moons?

"I have to get home," I said. I was hoping to catch Brandon before he left so I could see how he was doing. And I missed him.

"I don't want you walking home, Celeste. Or anywhere, for that matter. I think it's best that you are always around someone. And I think that someone should be me." Nash didn't speak with his usual confidence but rather with a soft, genuine quality.

"Please, I insist," he said. "I'll drive you." He even took my backpack from me and started walking toward his car.

"I thought you hated wolves," I said.

"I do—but I'd hate for you to be involved with one even more."

I hesitated in the doorway. "Just as friends," I called after him.

"Just as friends," he confirmed.

It was hard, knowing Nash as long as I had, to completely sever all ties with him. And I had been so busy with Brandon, I hadn't had the chance to miss Nash's friendship.

Brandon's Jeep was already gone. I'd have to seek him out as soon as possible.

I decided to work on my research that evening. I checked my notes and my calendar. The moon was waning, still weeks away from being full again. I reviewed my observations on our romantic date with the wolves, the time I saw Brandon in the woods by the gymnasium, and watching him turn. I included these new werewolf sightings in my calendar.

Unfortunately, my efforts to make contact with Brandon weren't going well. Brandon wasn't returning my calls or texts. I felt so awful for him, truly isolated from me, the other students, and now from the town. I wouldn't even be able to get to Dr. Meadows, who I knew was desperate to meet Brandon. Everything was getting so out of hand. I felt the world was caving in on us.

"It has to be wolves," my dad said at dinner about the werewolf sightings. I was like my father—skeptical about anything unfamiliar or not scientifically proven. But now I knew that a werewolf did exist and that he was being spotted by the local community.

"People don't have anything better to do than gossip," my mom said, referring to the town's rumors.

"After those wolves showed up at your school," my dad said, "I'm sure it put thoughts in people's minds."

"Everyone is talking about it," my mom chimed in.

"Make sure you don't walk home. Get a ride or I'll pick you up," my dad told me. "Call me anytime."

"I have to admit a few girls at work said they saw one, too," my mom added.

"I want you on a curfew," my dad said to me.

"What?"

"Just for the time being," he continued. "You've already had a run-in with a pack of wolves, and then they showed up at school. I don't want it to happen again."

"Dad!" I said.

"I don't want to be the bad guy here, but I have to put my foot down."

A curfew wasn't really something I needed, as I was always back home well in advance of any grounding possibilities. But I didn't like that the once-peaceful town was suddenly overridden with fear. It seemed full moons, folklore, and strange events were affecting not only me and Brandon but the entire town of Legend's Run.

TWENTY-SIX

missing pumpkin

"Meet me at Abby's," Ivy said when I answered my phone after dinner. "She said it's urgent."

"What is it?" I asked.

"I don't know, but she sounded upset. I told her we'd be right over."

When we arrived at Abby's, our friend was waiting outside on her porch. She was only slightly bundled up, and her breath was visible in the cool air.

"Pumpkin is missing," Abby said.

Pumpkin was Abby's five-year-old golden retriever with an orangey-rust coat and a white spot that looked like an earring on her left ear. Pumpkin was gentle and friendly and wasn't prone to running off.

"It's not like Pumpkin to stay away," she said anxiously.

"We can't find her!"

We began knocking on Ivy and Abby's neighbors' doors.

Abby was distraught. She was usually strong but today she was frazzled. She loved Pumpkin as much as I loved Champ, and I knew if Champ were missing, I'd be devastated, too.

Ivy and I tried to console her with talk of new fashion trends, but nothing was distracting her. We knocked on every door, asking if anyone had spotted her golden retriever.

After a few hours, exhausted, frozen, and dogless, we returned to Abby's house. We scarfed down pizza as we downloaded photos of Pumpkin on the computer and duplicated them on her dad's state-of-the-art jumbo home copier.

"We'll post these tomorrow," Ivy said, taking a stack with us.

"I really appreciate this," Abby said. "I miss her so much."

"I know she'll come home," Ivy said, giving her a hug.

"I bet she's somewhere safe," I said.

"I hope so," she said. "She's my best friend—besides you two, of course."

"Of course," Ivy and I agreed.

Ivy put the stack of pictures in the back of her car. Ivy was sweet and drove me back to my house.

"That dog is as good as dead, I'm afraid."

"Ivy!" I said, shocked at her morbid remark.

"I'm not trying to be heartless," she said. "It's just with roaming wolves and a werewolf on the loose, she should have kept her locked in the house."

Wolves were bad enough preying on defenseless felines. But a werewolf? My werewolf?

It couldn't be.

The following afternoon I went with Ivy, Abby, their boyfriends, and Nash to post Pumpkin's picture on every telephone pole and in every coffee shop. We hung our fliers next to ones for other dogs that had gone missing in the past few months. Any reason for Pumpkin's absence wasn't good, but to me, if Brandon was the reason—he'd be beside himself. He was devoted to animal rights and I'd seen how great he was with them—even wild animals. I was distracted by this concern, but as I didn't want to steal the focus from Abby's circumstances, I overcompensated by being lively and chatty with my friends.

"I know why you've been so happy today," Ivy said, taking me aside. "It's because of Nash. You are always so happy when you are with him."

"Really?" I asked.

"Yes."

I tried to analyze her diagnosis of my emotional state. In a way, my best friend was right. I knew we all had a blast hanging out as a sixsome, and there was incredible bliss in having a boyfriend. But I'd never felt such depths of feelings for Nash as I did for Brandon. And because Brandon was a Westsider—and now a werewolf—there were so many difficulties to our happiness together. I knew that no matter what, I could be happier with Brandon than I could be with Nash.

Ivy dropped me off at home and I saw a strange car waiting at the end of our street. I was opening our front door when someone got out and scurried toward me. I recognized the long gray hair pouring out from under a red hat.

"Dr. Meadows?" I said. I hurried toward her.

"Have you heard?" she said, breathless. "He's been discovered."

"Yes, everyone is spotting him. I'm really worried. And it's not even the full moon. What's happening?"

"I don't know, but I must see him, too."

"I am trying to convince him, but it's not easy. He's skeptical, and also really wants to keep his secret from the world."

"I know, but you must let me see him. It is imperative. If people are coming in contact with him—he could be in danger."

"I don't want him to be hurt—"

"If I don't get to him before someone else does, there could be dire consequences. No one is safe. That's all I know."

I didn't like Dr. Meadows's dramatics, but I knew her concern was real. And I feared for Brandon, too.

"If he doesn't come to me, I'll have to go to him," Dr. Meadows said urgently. "I won't be able to wait for your permission any longer. I will have to find him on my own."

"I want him to be cured and safe. That's all."

"Of course you do. You love him," she said in a soft voice. She drew my hair back from my face.

Dr. Meadows was the only one who knew my true feelings toward Brandon. I was surprised to find I felt relieved with someone else holding my secret.

"What happens if he kisses me," I asked, "when he's a . . . ?"

She paused with a cold, hard stare. "You mustn't. That is all I can tell you."

Dr. Meadows scurried away before I could say another word.

When I let myself into the house, Frank Sinatra was serenading me from my back pocket. I scrambled for my cell and hurried up to my room.

"Hello?"

"It's good to hear your voice."

"Yours, too."

"I miss you," Brandon said.

His words melted my heart.

"I miss you, too. How have you been?"

"Better. I'd prefer if I could see you at school—and after."

"I know—but you can. We can," I insisted.

"It's too risky. I've been overhearing students—"

"But if it's not a full moon, it can't be you."

"But what if it is? I dream I'm a wolf every night," he said, his voice filled with concern.

"It's only on a full moon that I've seen you turn. I've recorded everything in my notebook. You haven't tried to harm or scare anyone on the other nights."

"But I can't remember the other nights. So how do we really know?"

"What if it's a hoax? Someone trying to cash in on the werewolf folklore?"

"Or what if it's another werewolf?"

"Another one?" He sighed. "I'd hate for anyone else to be going through what I am."

"I don't want anyone to hurt you," I said.

"Me? That's not what I'm worried about."

Brandon was always concerned with others before himself. It was one of the traits that made him so alluring.

"I saw you with Nash. He's been doting on you lately."

"I'm not dating him," I assured Brandon.

"Yeah . . . but just seeing you together. It's hard. I want us to be the ones hanging out together."

"You do?" I wasn't totally sure of Brandon's wishes. I felt like he kept me at a distance, and I was afraid to stick my neck out too far.

"Of course I want to be with you. It's just . . . we have a few obstacles."

"If I hadn't gotten lost that day—" I lamented.

"I didn't mean that in any way—" he said sincerely. "I

know for some reason you blame yourself. I thought knowing Mr. Worthington's story, and getting my family's history, would make you feel better."

"But if I hadn't been lost in the woods, then you wouldn't have been bitten."

"And then I wouldn't have gotten the best brownies of my life."

A smile broke free from my frown. Brandon was brave in many ways. I admired his strength, and it felt impossible for me to feel anything for him but adoration.

My encounter with the Westside fortune-teller entered my mind. "Dr. Meadows . . . she might be coming for you."

"With a cure?"

"She keeps saying she has to see you first."

"Then that means she doesn't have one." He couldn't hide the disappointment in his voice.

"I just wanted to let you know. You might have a psychic stalker on your hands."

"The only stalker I want is you," he said.

"I'm doing my best."

"I have to go. It's almost sundown, but I wanted to call and let you know . . ."

"Yes?"

"That I can't stop thinking about you."

"Me, too. I want us to have that date in the woods again," I said.

"I do, too."

"You remember?"

"No, but I jotted down as much as I could when I woke up. I wrote down that the snow sparkled like diamonds in your hair."

That was all I needed. If Brandon took the time to jot down notes about me at the same time I was recording my memories, then it confirmed to me that our connection was real.

We got off the phone and I reveled in the fact that he was even more creative and dreamy than my overactive imagination could have imagined.

TWENTY-SEVEN
moonlight hideaway

Before English class started, Ivy and I chatted together as Dylan and Jake whispered to each other and acted like werewolves. Nash hung back and laughed.

My classmates snickered as the jocks roared and snarled.

"Have you seen the werewolf?" I heard someone ask Hayley Phillips.

"Doesn't seem like he's hitting the Westside," she retorted loud enough for Ivy and me to hear.

Dylan and Jake stopped showing off when Abby bolted into class.

"I was almost attacked last night," Abby said. "First my dog. Now me."

"What happened?" Ivy asked.

"Are you okay?" I wondered.

"After volleyball practice, I left the school gym and this *thing* jumped out of the bushes at me."

"What thing?" Ivy asked.

"A thing! A creature."

"You have to be kidding me," Ivy said. "A creature?"

Dylan sat by her and consoled her. "Abby, it might be best if you kept quiet."

"Did it touch you?" I asked, concerned.

"No—" she said. "I screamed so loud I think I scared it away."

"What did it look like?" I asked.

"It was evil, that's all I know. All I saw was dark hair and fangs."

I turned to Brandon. Distress showed on his face. He put his head in his maimed hand and flipped through a textbook.

Mrs. Clark entered the classroom. "Everyone, take your seats. You'll be reading your essays aloud in class today."

"Abby says she saw the werewolf last night here at school," Heidi Rosen said.

Abby turned to her in horror.

"Is there something you'd like to report?" Mrs. Clark asked.

"Yes," Abby said. "Just like Heidi, I saw the Legend's Run Werewolf."

Heidi glared at Abby as the rest of the students snickered again.

I couldn't concentrate on any of the murmuring in the classroom. Brandon wouldn't be so brazen as to scare Abby. And if he did, what would I do? I wasn't sure I should feel affection toward a guy who was scaring my friends. But Brandon never hurt me or posed a threat when we were together, so why would he do that to others? It just didn't make sense.

After class was over, I tried to catch up to Brandon, but he snuck out quickly and slipped away into the crowd of students. I seemed to be the only one at Legend's Run High who couldn't spot the werewolf.

Later, Ivy and I were in the library gossiping during study hall.

"Do you believe Abby really saw a werewolf?" Ivy asked me.

Really, I thought she did. But how could I tell Ivy that?

"I'm not sure," I said instead. "I think she thinks she saw something. But do you really think a werewolf is running around Legend's Run?" I asked her.

"I still think there was something bizarro about that wolfman Brandon Maddox and that incident with the wolves. Maybe it's him."

I paused. "Does Brandon have fangs?"

"I don't know. I haven't made a point of getting that close to him."

"You really think he's a werewolf?" I pressed.

"I swear I saw him stare at those wolves and they were staring right back at him. It's possible. He is from the Westside," she said with a laugh.

I didn't think my best friend's comment was funny.

"But I think that's it," Ivy continued as if she just realized something. "Ever since I said that thing about Brandon being weird when the wolves came, Abby's had to top me. With her dog missing, and now this crazy story. Don't you see it?"

"I'm not sure I follow."

"I think Abby's just trying to get attention," she said, fixated on our friend. "Everyone wants to know her story about seeing a werewolf."

I didn't reply but listened to my friend rant.

"Did you see at lunch the way Dylan and Jake were fawning all over her? And Nash, though he was just hanging back, taking it all in."

I was surprised at Ivy's being jealous of the attention Abby was receiving.

"If she did see something—" I said.

"She didn't see anything, don't you get it? She's made the whole thing up. Just to get attention. It's so like her."

"You're saying Abby lied?"

Just then Abby returned to the library from her locker.

"This is just between us," Ivy said.

"Of course," I said.

"What did I miss?" Abby said. She always felt left out

when Ivy and I were together. In this case, her feelings were accurate.

After school, I was heading down the stairs when I spotted Brandon. He was standing at the bottom of the landing, out of the way of students. I was startled and surprised he was finally making contact with me.

"I have to ask you to come over," he said quickly when I reached him. "It's important."

Normally, I would have been happy that we'd be together again. But his tone was more stern than romantic.

"I'll be there," I said.

For a brief moment, we locked eyes—his royal blues glistening like raindrops. It was obvious he couldn't linger like he longed to, but whatever it was he needed to tell me was more important than risking a secret stairwell kiss.

He escaped into the hallway before I could convince him to stay any longer.

As I drove from the Eastside to the Westside, I was struck by the number of flyers there were about missing dogs. I couldn't even count the signs that were taped to the telephone poles along the road. Was a wolf—or werewolf—in fact harming the dogs of Legend's Run?

My heart pounded as I drove my car along the Maddoxes' private drive and past the frozen pond where we'd shared our romantic ice skate together. I wondered what Brandon wanted to tell me. I found him pacing by his guesthouse. I hopped out of the car and raced up to him.

"I've become a danger," he said. "Everyone is spotting me now."

"I haven't seen you—I still think people are just paranoid, scared of the wolves that showed up at school."

"How can I know when I don't remember anything?" He raked his hands through his hair in frustration. "Your friend Abby. She said I jumped out at her."

"You haven't hurt anyone—they're just scared." I tried to ease his mind. "Besides, there's no full moon. You're not transforming into a werewolf."

"But does that matter anymore? I don't know what I'll do next. It's in my blood—just like Mr. Worthington—Charlie—told me. No one in town is safe from me after sunset."

"But, Brandon—"

"I can't remember anything I do at night. I know I'm the one responsible. The only way to cure this is . . ."

We both paused. I wasn't sure what Brandon's resolution was going to be and I wasn't about to hear it. I stared at him squarely in the face, fear and anger tearing through me. "Not a silver bullet!" I said. "That isn't the solution! And if you think that for a minute—"

"No," he said, breaking a smile. "I'd like a cure that doesn't involve bullets."

I breathed out a huge sigh.

"But since we don't have a cure . . ."

"What are you going to do?" One fear was replaced with another. I could only imagine the love of my life pushing himself further away from me and the town. "Are you going to leave?"

"No, the idea is to stay. Confined. For the whole night."

"What do you mean?"

"My grandparents have gone to Florida for a vacation, so they won't even miss me."

"Miss you? Where are you going?"

"I'll need your help." He put a heavy-duty padlock in my hand.

"What am I supposed to do with this?"

"I rigged this today," he said, pointing to several brackets and a latch on the outside of the guesthouse. "All you have to do is put the lock on just before the sun sets. I don't think I can bust it. And if I do, at least we tried."

"But you'll be locked inside your room all night?"

"That's the idea."

"What if something happens and you need help? You'll be trapped."

"I'll call nine-one-one. I have a phone and all the amenities I need. I'll be fine. It's the people of Legend's Run I'm worried about."

"This isn't any way to live, Brandon—like a caged animal."

"I don't have a choice, Celeste." He cupped my face in his hands.

We sat together in the guesthouse, snuggled together on top of his single bed. I caressed the scar on his hand and snuck in as many kisses as I could before nightfall. The sun began setting behind the trees.

"It's time," he said.

"But I don't want to leave."

"I'm afraid you have to. You can't stay in here with me."

Brandon gave me a long kiss and shooed me out the door.

"I'll come back before school," I said.

"Just remember the key," he said. "I don't want to get detention for being late."

As the sun continued to set, he closed the door.

Using all my strength, I pressed the padlock closed. I tugged at it several times, making sure it had truly latched.

I leaned against the door, placing my palm on it. It was as if I could feel Brandon's energy coming through from the other side.

"You better go," he finally said.

"I don't want to. You'll be all alone."

"It's better than the alternative," he said.

"I'll have my phone with me at all times," I assured him. "Please call me."

"See you in the morning," he said. "Hopefully I'll still be here."

I drove off down the long driveway. My stomach felt hollow, leaving Brandon all alone locked away in his room.

It was one thing when he was hidden away in the woods. But to me, this was worse.

My true love was jailed—by his condition and by his own free will.

the wolf whisperer

The next few nights I continued to secure Brandon at sunset and free him in the morning before school. As much as I hated for him to be locked away, I did enjoy waking up, rushing over to Riverside, and seeing him first thing in the morning. He was always so gorgeous. His hair was messy like a model's, and his eyes always glistened like the moon. I had never woken up so happy in my life.

At night, though, it was different. I felt a huge pain in my soul whenever Brandon closed his door. My friends insisted I attend the basketball games or go out with them and Nash. I had to admit I was torn. There was nothing I enjoyed more than being with my friends except for one thing—being with Brandon. And if Brandon hadn't entered the picture, I'm sure I'd still be content sipping hot chocolate on the bleachers with my friends and watching the basketball being passed back and forth by the hot athletes at Legend's Run High. Nash being interested in me *was* flattering. But now I saw another side of Legend's Run that no other Eastsider saw. And it—or, rather, he—was hard to forget.

I didn't know how I was ever going to tell my best friends I favored a fingerless-glove-wearing Westsider over their best friend, a popular all-star. Not only would I be disappointing the two girls who mattered most to me, but I'd be upsetting the balance of popularity that they strove so hard to achieve.

But Brandon's plan was working and he seemed pleased with the results: The werewolf spottings decreased immediately.

I wondered if he'd have to be locked away inside his guest-house forever.

One morning after I opened Brandon's door, I noticed several dogs snooping around the grass by the birdbath. One was a golden retriever.

"I didn't know your grandparents had so many dogs," I said. "I only saw the husky in the window."

"They don't. We only have one dog."

"But there's, like, three over there by the birdbath. And one looks just like Pumpkin, Abby's dog that's missing."

"You think it might be?" Brandon asked. "My grandma was telling me she keeps finding stray dogs in the yard."

I walked behind the main house and noticed a white

terrier, a Great Dane, a poodle, and several mutts scurrying around, barking and playing.

I raced over to the golden retriever and examined the dog's left ear. Behind some dirt and a few pieces of brush was a white circle. "This is Pumpkin. She has a white mark on her ear!"

"I don't know where they came from, but they are always here in the morning. Every few days a new dog. My grandmother has already called a few owners and they've come for them. But a few days later, new ones arrive. If they don't have tags, we've been taking care of them. But it's been weird. I feel like they are . . ."

"Following you?" I asked. "Like the wolves?"

He smiled as he looked at his brood of furry admirers.

"I knew you weren't destroying people's pets. Instead you were taking caring of them."

Brandon beamed.

"I can't believe this, Brandon! You found Pumpkin!" I petted my friend's dog and snuggled her cute canine face against mine. "She's been missing for a week. We posted signs all over town."

"All over town? I didn't see any."

"Well, along the Eastside." I felt ashamed. "I think we've learned a lesson here. But I have to tell Abby!" I said excitedly. I pulled my phone out from my purse and called my friend.

"Guess who I have?" I asked in a playful tone.

"I don't know," Abby said in a groggy voice. "It's too early for jokes."

"It starts with a *P*," I hinted.

There was silence on the other end.

I took a picture of Pumpkin and sent it to Abby's phone. I could almost hear her screams coming from the east side of town.

When I arrived at English class, Abby came in and gave me another hug. She'd been squeezing me all morning long, and since she was so toned, I was starting to cave in.

"I'm getting bruises," I said.

Nash, Jake, and Dylan were hanging out by our desks.

"Abby told me Brandon Maddox found her," Ivy said.

"He did," I said.

"How did he find her—and more important, how did you find out?"

"Yes," Nash said, "how did you find that out from Brandon?"

"Uh . . ." I was going to tell them the same story I told Abby. "I saw Brandon with Pumpkin. And he told me that if we had put signs on the Westside, she would have been returned sooner."

"Are you sure he didn't steal her?" Nash asked.

"Why would he? He already has a dog."

"How do you know that?" Ivy asked skeptically.

Just then Brandon walked into class. We all turned to

him. Abby rose and went straight over to him.

"I want to thank you so much for finding my dog," she said sweetly.

Then she did the unimaginable. Abby Kensington leaned over and hugged Brandon Maddox in front of the entire English class.

Dylan folded his arms. Ivy gasped. I high-fived the air. Nash shook his head.

Brandon appeared more surprised than any of us as Abby returned to her seat.

"See, I told you he's not so bad," I said to my friends. Brandon passed and gave me a quick smile before taking his seat. Nash gave me a stern glare, and he and his teammates sat down.

"He is handsome underneath all those layers of hair," Ivy said, obviously not wanting Abby to show her up.

The bell rang and Mrs. Clark called the names of those who were to share a brief synopsis of their essay with the class. My stomach sank when I heard her say "Celeste Parker."

I wasn't crazy about speaking in front of others. I had participated in some school plays but never as the lead. Most of the students were nice, but I liked when everyone stared at the teacher and not at me.

Nash seemed proud of me, standing in front of the class. For the first time, I was the star instead of him. It made me feel empowered that he seemed so pleased. I saw Ivy and Abby, who were smiling at me and both giving me the thumbs-up.

Then I caught sight of Brandon and my paper shook slightly in my hand.

"Werewolves," I said.

"That's a timely subject," Mrs. Clark said.

"In many centuries and societies, people swear they've seen a man who takes the form of a wolf. Others insist the werewolf, like the unicorn, is a figment of man's imagination.

"Throughout time, werewolves have been part of many different cultures' folklore. That might be a kind of mythology to explain abnormal behavior if one is not behaving appropriately for their community. But others believe that the werewolf is not folklore or fiction. I even interviewed a man who claims one of his ancestors was a werewolf.'

The students perked up.

"He told me that the bite of a wolf can transform a human into a werewolf and that the affliction can be carried through man's blood from one generation to another. The person with the link to the wolves can transform once under a full moon. He says there is truth in the stories of the Legend's Run Werewolf."

"Ooooh!" I heard someone say.

"I saw him," Abby shouted out. Other classmates shushed her.

"Many students believe they've seen him," I continued. "And I think I've seen him, too."

"Do you have pictures?" someone asked.

Mrs. Clark tapped her desk with her pencil.

"But I'd like to put forth one theory that isn't popular among the rumors. Just because one takes the lycan form doesn't mean that they prey on others. They, too, might have a soul. When the full moon is over, they might want to be treated just like you or me."

My class applauded me, and as I sat down Brandon gave me an approving wink.

"Someone has footage of the werewolf," my mom called from the family room before dinner. "It's going to be on the five o'clock news."

I raced downstairs. If Brandon was in seclusion, this couldn't be him. Did he break out?

"It's going to be on in a minute," my mom said when I plopped down on the floor in front of the TV.

Megan Crumley, our local news reporter, was standing outside Penny for Your Thoughts. "Channel Eleven has just learned that Dr. Camille Meadows from Riverside Township has discovered a werewolf and captured it on film," she began. "As you may have heard, many residents have been claiming they've witnessed an unusual creature roaming Legend's Run at night, and many are calling this creature the Wolfman.

"With all the werewolf sightings, no one has been able to prove its existence," she continued.

Dr. Meadows had warned me if I didn't bring Brandon to her, she'd go to him. But why wouldn't she tell me she found him? Why would she go to our local news station first?

"How were you able to find him?" the reporter asked.

"I sensed it," Dr. Meadows said. "I have paranormal abilities and I used them to guide me. I finally got this last week."

My heart plummeted. All along, Dr. Meadows had been trying to use Brandon for her own gain.

"Is that the psychic you spent your allowance on?" my mom asked.

I held my breath and covered my mouth.

The film was grainy and dark at best. It looked like it had been filmed with a phone as opposed to a high-end video camera. At first it was out of focus. There was the sound of rustling in the woods. A figure lurked behind a tree; wild and long black hair covered its face. It howled like a wolf. Then the figure dashed out of view. The camera followed, shining its light on several bare trees. Suddenly a sturdy hand swung at the camera. There was scrambling as we could hear heavy breathing and the camera pointed to the ground as Dr. Meadows ran away.

"Well, that certainly looks like something to me," the anchor said. "What, I'm not sure, but you can decide. Click on our website and tell us your thoughts. Wolfman or Prankman?"

"Replay that," I said. "I want to see something."

I grabbed the remote and rewound the clip. I played it slowly, examining it closely.

"What are you looking for?" my mom asked.

The figure swiped at the camera with its right hand. However, when I reviewed it, there wasn't a scar. No sign of a wolf bite to be seen. It wasn't Brandon. But that realization raised as many questions as it answered.

TWENTY-NINE

werewolf tv

After my mom went to her scrapbooking party, I headed for Brandon's in a hurry.

"I was on the news," he said as soon as I got out of the car.

"But it couldn't have been you. There wasn't a scar on your right hand."

"What?"

"I slowed down the footage on the TV," I said. "When this creature swiped at the camera, there wasn't a scar." I took Brandon's right palm and showed him. "See? You have a major one."

"How do you know?" he asked, not convinced by my theory. "Maybe it disappears when I turn. I don't remember."

"But I do remember, and it doesn't."

"Are you sure? If it wasn't me, then what was it—or who? Another werewolf?"

"Maybe. Or maybe it was some kids playing jokes. I don't know. I just know it wasn't you."

Brandon breathed a sigh of relief. He placed his arm around my shoulder and drew me into him.

"I've never met anyone like you," he said.

"The sun is setting," I warned. "What do you want to do now?"

"I can't stay in that box forever. I don't know what to do."

I hugged him.

"And more important, Celeste, how are we going to be together?"

"Maybe it's time you go back to the way you were living. Free, like anyone else. Werewolf or not."

"I'm not sure . . . I'd rather not take any chances."

I admired Brandon's values. With everything he had to worry about, the first thing on his mind was the well-being of the town.

Brandon kissed me tenderly, and I fought off my incredible desire to be locked away all night with him inside his safe house.

As another full moon approached, I met Ivy, Abby, their beaux, and Nash at Wings and Things. If I couldn't be on the end of Brandon's lips, then at least I would be surrounded by my friends.

"That's what I saw," Abby insisted to Ivy when I arrived at their table. "I swear."

"That wasn't a werewolf," Ivy charged. "Werewolves have hair all over their faces."

No they don't, I wanted to say. Brandon sported a handsome goatee.

"Well, this one didn't," Abby stated. "I don't know why you don't believe me."

Ivy paused. "I do. Not that I believe in werewolves, but I believe you saw something," she said sincerely.

I thought Ivy had finally realized that the whole werewolf thing was putting a strain on her relationship with Abby. And she was all about keeping us together as a friendly unit.

"Where have you been?" Ivy asked me.

"I had a million things to do."

"Did you see the werewolf on TV?" Abby asked. My friends were already well into their wings, so I got to pick at their leftovers.

"Yes. Did it look like a hoax to you?" Ivy asked.

"I'm not sure," I said truthfully. I knew it wasn't Brandon, but I didn't know if there was someone else turning at nightfall when the full moon had waned. "I only know it wasn't any of us, since we're all here after sunset."

"I still think that Brandon Maddox might have something to do with this," Ivy observed.

Abby's face lit up. "Maybe it is him. Maybe the Legend's Run Werewolf is Brandon."

Everyone paused.

"I told you," Ivy said. "I saw him stare at those wolves. It wasn't like anything I've seen on *Animal Planet*. This was like something Dr. Meadows would do."

"There you go again," Jake said. "I think you must have a thing for that guy. It's all you ever talk about . . . Brandon and the wolves."

"Well, he's also saving dogs," Abby said. "If he is a werewolf, he's a good one."

"What do you think, Celeste?" Ivy asked. "You're always defending the underdog."

"I guess you figured it out. Brandon Maddox is a werewolf."

They all laughed, and this time I did, too.

"Either way, there is something strange going on and it's best we all stick together," Nash encouraged.

"Speaking of that . . ." Ivy said, "we have to go, but Nash can drive you home."

As if on cue, Abby, Jake, Dylan, and Ivy rose while Nash remained seated.

"I thought you were driving me home," I said under my breath.

"This way you and Nash can have some alone time now that you guys are back together."

"Back together?" I asked.

"Since this werewolf thing, he has really been there for you," Ivy said. "It's just like old times."

My friends paid the bill, and Nash and I got into his car. He even opened the door for me. The way he was suddenly being a gentleman was endearing. But I felt awkward as he drove me home. Though he was usually self-centered, I knew there was an inner side to him that he didn't share with other girls. He parked in front of my house.

"Celeste—" he said.

The car was dark, which only added to the appeal of his handsome features. Normally, he would have leaned into me and I would have gotten a melt-worthy kiss.

But since we'd broken up, we hadn't shared any romantic gestures.

"Yes?" I finally said.

Nash pulled off his class ring. "I want you to have this," he said.

It was sweet. Nash was attractive, by any girl's standards. If this had happened a few months ago, I would have taken it without missing a beat. But I wasn't going to commit to Nash. Even if it were the smart thing to do, even if it didn't make sense to love a guy who I couldn't see at night and couldn't be embraced by in front of my friends by day. But my heart had been taken by such a guy, and I couldn't go against it.

He held out the ring and it shone under the streetlight.

"You can try it on," he said. "It may need to be resized."

I felt so bad. Nash was my friend, but I couldn't give him my heart, and I couldn't take his ring.

"There is a part of me that wants this ring, Nash," I said.

"I'd be the luckiest girl at school."

He scooted closer to me and I looked away.

"But . . ." he said.

"I'm just not—"

"I've seen this in movies," he said. Nash wasn't used to being turned down. He wasn't the kind of guy who rejection was likely to happen to. It tore me up inside to be the one who hurt him—especially since I cared about him.

"I'm not saying I don't care for you. You know I do," I said.

"I know," he said. "I'll just give you some more time."

Nash wasn't used to losing. He made a point of letting me know the game wasn't over yet.

However, in his frustration, he reached to unzip his duffel bag and threw the ring into it.

I saw something dark and hairy coming out of the bag. I screamed.

"What?" he said. He jumped back, too.

"It's a squirrel!" I pressed my whole body against the passenger-side door.

He, too, scooted away. He quickly opened his car door and jumped out. The overhead car light illuminated the inside. Something furry was sticking out of his duffel bag.

"That—" I said. "It's alive!"

"This?" he said, pointing to the bag. "It's nothing."

I peered into the bag and grabbed the dark fur. He tried to stop my hand, but it was too late. I pulled out a wild wig.

"It's an old Halloween costume. Here—" he said, stuffing it back into his bag. "Let me walk you to the door."

Nash had never walked me to the door before. He just didn't want me to see the costume inside the duffel bag, but it was too late.

I got out of the car, and he met me on the sidewalk.

"It was you," I said.

He smiled sheepishly. "Me? What?"

"All along."

He continued to grin a boyish grin.

"Scaring Heidi. And Abby? Being on TV?"

He looked like he couldn't tell if I was going to hug him or slug him. I didn't do either. Instead I just shook my head.

"I did it for you," he said.

"I don't understand—"

"It brought you to me. We've been hanging out together like old times. We've been so happy, all of us together. And you and I . . . It's just like when we first went out. I told you I'd show you that you needed me, Celeste. I just had to show you how much."

I was furious. Nash had put the entire town on alert and caused Brandon to be locked away for weeks. But then I realized the lengths to which Nash had gone to get my attention. We were hanging out as a sixsome again. For some reason, I was the only one who saw the fear in Nash's face and knew that there was another layer to his superjock image. I knew that is why he needed me more than he needed the other girls at school, and I had to admit that it was nice to be needed.

"Why couldn't you have just been thoughtful, Nash?" I asked. "That's all I ever wanted from you. I just wanted you to really be interested in me and the things I care about. You didn't have to pretend to be a werewolf so you could be the hero."

He took my hands in his. "But it worked, didn't it? We're practically back together."

Before I could step away, he drew me into him and kissed me.

I turned and wiped my mouth off.

He smiled at the success of his ruse.

"This will remain between the two of us?" he asked.

"There's no one I want to tell," I said.

"This is my biggest prank yet," he said proudly. "I might want to reveal it myself."

a night to remember

I was so let down by Dr. Meadows's and Nash's antics. It was one thing if Dr. Meadows had been unable to help me or Brandon, but what kind of doctor was she when she only wanted to help herself? All this time I was searching for a cure, while she was searching for celebrity. And ultimately, she wound up finding the wrong werewolf.

Nash, who had been the biggest crush of my life and my first boyfriend, had cooked up his scheme to get me to run back into his arms. It was flattering that he had gone to so much trouble for us to be together. But his foolish trick to get me back, which caused so much stress for other people, just proved why we weren't meant to be a couple.

* * *

The following day was the first of a full moon. Just after sunset, I hurried over to Riverside to tell the one person who needed to know the most about Nash's prank. I hoped I could convince Brandon it was time for him to return to his normal yet unusual nightlife because he wasn't doing anyone any harm.

I knocked on his door. "Brandon! It's me."

"Celeste?" he asked from the other side. "What are you doing here?"

The heavy door separated us, but I was going to put an end to that.

"I'm coming in." I unlocked the lock and opened his guesthouse door. I found Brandon pacing inside in his werewolf form.

I was so drawn to him I rushed into his arms. I immediately felt warmed by his embrace and safe and happy in his presence.

"Nash was the one on TV, not you," I blurted out.

"He was the werewolf everyone has been spotting?" Brandon asked.

"Yes."

"You're kidding."

"No, he was," I said with a laugh.

"And this is the guy you date?"

"I used to date. I guess he meant well, though," I defended. "He was doing it so he and I could get back together," I confessed. "He thought he was doing the right thing."

"It's your nature to see the good in people, isn't it?" He

brushed my hair away from my face.

"I don't know—"

"So, did it work?" he asked, stepping back. "Are you back together with him? Is that why you are here?"

"No—" I said, and pulled him close. "I'm here to be with you. And to tell you that it's time for you to be who you really are."

I took him by the hand and led him outside. The full moon glowed brightly in the night sky. Brandon inhaled a huge breath of fresh air. His sights and senses perked up. He was finally free.

We walked hand in hand up the side of the hilltop into his favorite outdoor spot.

"I know that I want us to be together under any conditions," I said, looking up at him. Brandon and I locked gazes. His lips were only inches from mine. It was pure torture.

"I want to kiss you so badly," I said. "But as you are . . . now. I was warned against it. I just don't know what it'll do to you."

"Or you?" he said, concerned.

Our foreheads touched and our arms wrapped around each other's neck.

"It's okay, Celeste," he said. "Either way, I love you."

I looked up at him again and paused as if I'd just frozen in the snow. The woods were eerily quiet. "What did you say?" I asked again, wondering if I had heard Brandon correctly.

He stared down at me. His intensely alluring gray eyes

burned through me like ice. His wildly savage hair rested softly on his shoulders. His goateed face was unbelievably handsome, and his lips were magnetic.

"I love you," he said.

His words sent fiery tingles dancing down my spine. I wasn't sure if I'd just gone to heaven.

"I love you, too," I said. It was like a huge weight had lifted from me. He smiled a brilliant smile.

Brandon cupped my face in his maimed hand. We gazed at each other. Our connection was hypnotic. I was irresistibly drawn to him.

I had to kiss Brandon because I knew that if I didn't, I wouldn't be able to breathe. I'd never loved someone or something as much as I did him, and I knew at that moment I had to let him know how much.

"I want to kiss you. Now. But I'm afraid of hurting you more—"

"You don't have to be afraid," he said. "I'm already a werewolf. What could be worse?" He finally took me into his arms and did what I'd been waiting for him to do since I first saw him standing by the tree in the woods. He leaned into me and kissed me with such desire and intensity it was like nothing I'd ever experienced.

His lips were full and tender. The kiss was electric, seductively shocking. My whole body was electrified as tingles ran down my flesh and inside my veins.

We broke away and I melted into his embrace. I gazed

up and saw the full moon above me. Then Brandon noticed it, too.

He hid me from the moonlight and checked my hands and face.

"What have I done?" he asked. "I'll never forgive myself!"

"But I haven't been bitten. Maybe nothing will happen to me. I'm more afraid for you," I said.

He held me in his arms again. It was the most magical kiss of my life, and I was still hoping for more.

I didn't know if there would be consequences for not heeding Dr. Meadows's warning. But for now, there were more hazards in not kissing this guy, this werewolf, the love of my life.

I was afraid to sleep. I dreaded waking up the next day with a beard and hairy legs. On Brandon, the werewolf traits were powerful and alluring. But I couldn't imagine them being so attractive on a girl. My fate would be I'd end up traveling with a circus.

I lay awake all night long. Replaying in my mind was the kiss on the lips of a werewolf. When would we know the effects of that kiss? Did I have to wait for a full moon to turn or just any moon? Or would it be the end of Brandon?

The next day Brandon wasn't in school. I waited all day, hoping at any moment he'd walk through the classroom door, I'd spot him in the hallway, or he'd show up in the cafeteria. But I knew better, and my stomach was filled with anxiety. I'd once again caused unlikely events to unfold, the effects at this point unknown. I'd defied once again Dr. Meadows's warning. This could only mean one thing—trouble.

Nash and Ivy were concerned with my being distracted.

"Why are you so miserable?" Ivy asked. "You didn't even eat your lunch."

I was worried sick.

"I think I should keep an eye on you," Nash said. "You aren't yourself." He did his best to follow me around school, but no amount of silly jokes could break my distressed mood.

I was so afraid I'd hurt Brandon by our kiss underneath the full moon. I could think of nothing else.

The sun hovered over the treetops as I raced to Brandon's house. I called out his name and searched his small guesthouse, but I didn't hear or discover him. Then I headed for his hilltop. I couldn't wait to see him again.

I stepped over trees and trudged through the snow.

"Brandon," I called. "Brandon! Where are you?" My heart was aching. Where had Brandon gone? I feared that there were consequences to our kiss—and since nothing had happened to me, surely something had happened to him. Was he hurt, or worse? I couldn't bear to think about it any longer.

Suddenly a figure stepped out from behind a tree.

"Brandon?" I froze.

But was this the same Brandon I'd kissed the night before? Or was I being met by a menacing werewolf? Maybe it was foolish or even unsafe of me to have come here without knowing.

"Brandon?" I asked again, breathless.

"I still can't believe it," he said. He stepped out of the shadows in his handsome human form, but I still wasn't sure if it was safe to approach him.

"Believe what?"

He took my hands in his. His fingers were cold, but he seemed somehow refreshed and happier than I'd ever seen him.

"I told you something last night," he said. "Do you remember?"

"Yes," I said.

"But more important you told me something."

"Yes."

"Something that comes from the heart? That only real lovers say?"

I nodded exuberantly.

"Then it's true," he said, and gave me a hug. "This time it wasn't a dream I could barely remember."

"You remember?"

"Everything!" he said.

"I remember everything from the first night I was turned," he said, ecstatic. "I remember our first official date, with the snow glistening in your hair and Champ and the wolves playing together. I remember wanting to kiss you every time I saw you and how it took all my strength not to.

"And most important, Celeste, I remember the words you told me last night and the best kiss of my life."

We hugged and laughed and kissed.

"Then why would Dr. Meadows warn me against it?" I asked.

Brandon thought for a moment. "There was something magical about that kiss. That you cared for me in werewolf form . . . it brought my two worlds together. I'm sure there are some werewolves who don't want to remember anything that happens in the moonlight," he said with conviction. "But I'm not one of those."

We heard a car pulling into Brandon's drive in the distance.

"I guess my grandparents are home," he said.

Then Brandon ignored the car and kissed me. "I'm so glad I can remember," he said. "Because you are too good to forget."

We kissed again, and within a few moments the sun had set behind us. I heard a rustling in the woods. I thought I saw a pair of eyes watching us. "I think a wolf is following us," I said.

Brandon perked up. "It's not a wolf. I think there's some-one watching us," he said, concerned.

"Then we'll leave," I said. But it was too late. I saw an odd look in Brandon's eyes.

"I'm burning up," he said.

"No—" I cried. "Not now. What if it's your grandparents?"

I gazed back into the woods, hoping I'd see who or what was staring at us.

"It can't be them," Brandon said, frazzled. "They would have said something by now." He retreated deeper into the woods. "I'm changing."

"You can't—not if someone's out there!" I warned. I trailed Brandon farther into the brush. But Brandon was already taking off his jersey.

I heard branches cracking as if someone was following us.

I tried to hide Brandon behind a tree when I heard a branch snap a few yards away.

"Please," I begged Brandon, who was wincing in discomfort. "Not now!"

Brandon's eyes had turned red.

"No—" I cried, trying to cover his face with my hands. "What if someone is videotaping you?"

His hair grew shoulder length before me, and tiny dark hairs covered his arms and athletic chest.

"Please—don't!" I said to him. "It could be a hunter!"

I was afraid for Brandon's life and did my best to hide him with my arms.

"Oh no! You have to stop!" I said.

There was a goatee and stubble along his face where none had been. Fangs pierced out between the parting of his lips.

Brandon breathed heavily and I could see his senses were keened in on movement in the brush a few yards away.

"Please, whoever you are! Please, go away!" I shouted.

Brandon stepped in front of me. He wasn't about to let me take a silver bullet for him.

Just then a beam of light shone on Brandon. It was coming from only a few yards away. As Brandon retreated I noticed a figure holding a flashlight—and on his finger was a familiar class ring.

Several wolves howled in the distance. The light shining on Brandon quivered. Brandon howled in return, and the flashlight fell to the ground.

We heard a rustling in the woods away from us as if someone was running for their life. In the distance a car door slammed and an engine started. Squealing tires peeled off.

I stared at Brandon, who was as gorgeous as I'd ever seen him. I was scared, frightened of what was going to happen to us now. Brandon reached out and took my shaking hand in his steady and firm one. I felt an immediate surge of love and strength flow straight to my heart.

"What do we do now?" I asked him as the moon shone above us.

"We do something we couldn't do for many months," he replied in a sexy voice. "Something I'll always remember."

Brandon drew me into him and playfully nuzzled his stubbly cheek against mine and then nibbled my neck softly with his fangs. Then he kissed me with the roaring passion of a pack of werewolves and the romance of many full moons.

ACKNOWLEDGMENTS

I am so grateful to these wonderful people:

Katherine Tegen, who has made my dreams come true, and for invaluable advice in continuing to guide my writing career.

Ellen Levine, for your amazing direction, kindness, and everything you do.

Sarah Shumway, for your suggestions, humor, and friendship.

I'd like to thank my wonderful mom; my awesome brothers, Mark and Ben, my in-laws, Jerry, Hatsy, Hank, Wendy, Emily, and Max; and my best friends, Linda and Indigo.

Beware of a *kiss* under the full moon . . . it will change your life forever.